"Tonight is all we have left. Let's not waste a minute."

Misguided though Angela was, Jack pushed the dress down over her hips until it pooled at her feet. He'd let her believe that this was their last night together if that's what made her happy. Only *he* knew how he'd developed a craving for her that couldn't be satisfied in a weekend—or that he planned to make love to her so thoroughly she wouldn't have the power to leave.

She walked into the bedroom and he followed, stopping in the threshold to watch her climb onto the bed with the grace of a lioness. He tore away his pants and shirt, then slid in beside her, grabbing her wrists and trapping them above her head. Kissing a path from her mouth to her breasts, he inhaled her spiced scent. "You're so perfect. Are you ready for me?" he asked. His mouth traveled lower, hovering at the top of her thighs, and his hands eased her legs farther apart.

"Jack, I…"

"You're so sweet and slick." With teasing flicks of his tongue, he sent her over the edge.

"Jack, please." She cried out as spasms rocked her body. "Don't stop, Jack. Please don't stop," she moaned.

Jack chuckled and raised himself over her. "I don't intend to stop, Angela. Not until dawn. Maybe not even then."

Dear Reader,

Bold. Sexy. Sassy. Women who want. Men who provide. Those aspects of Harlequin Temptation intrigued me the first time I read one. So basic, yet so complex, the lure of these novels proved irresistible when I happened upon the right story.

At my ten-year high school reunion, I was amazed at how many of my classmates had married each other. However, a few high school sweethearts not only hadn't reunited, they were also still *very* available. The writer in me instantly started speculating about the possibilities…and Angela and Jack, my couple in *Seducing Sullivan*, came to life.

From the start, these two characters demanded a highly sensual story. When Harlequin launched BLAZE, Temptation's series of "red-hot" reads, my hopes for this story soared. Luckily, my editor had the same vision. She encouraged me to pull out all the stops in exploring Jack's and Angela's unresolved desires—and the results nearly scorched my computer keys!

Writing for Temptation is a dream come true for me. Be sure to watch for my next Temptation novel, another BLAZE title, available next year.

Sincerely,

Julie Elizabeth Leto

P.S. I'd love to gauge your reactions to *Seducing Sullivan.* Write to me at: Harlequin Books, 225 Duncan Mill Road, Don Mills, Ontario, Canada M3B 3K9.

It's hot…and it's out of control!

Don't miss the next BLAZE:
#689 BLACK VELVET by Carrie Alexander (July 1998)

SEDUCING SULLIVAN
Julie Elizabeth Leto

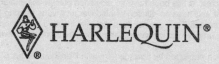

TORONTO • NEW YORK • LONDON
AMSTERDAM • PARIS • SYDNEY • HAMBURG
STOCKHOLM • ATHENS • TOKYO • MILAN • MADRID
PRAGUE • WARSAW • BUDAPEST • AUCKLAND

For my husband, Tim Klapka,
for supporting my writing from the beginning...
and for helping with the "research."

ISBN 0-373-25786-4

SEDUCING SULLIVAN

Copyright © 1998 by Julie Leto Klapka.

1

ANGELA HARRIS placed one manicured nail between her teeth, aching to bite the scarlet enamel. She thought she'd cured herself of the habit years ago. But old ways died hard, especially when she stood outside her ten-year reunion staring at an eighteen-by-twenty-seven enlargement of a picture Jack Sullivan had taken of her at their first high school dance.

"It's like staring in a mirror, isn't it?"

Jack's deep, resonant voice drifted past the soft background music and chatter coming from the ballroom behind him. On a current of wine-sweetened breath, his words swept over her bare shoulder and caressed the sensitive shell of her ear. Her jaw slackened, releasing her captive nail from her teeth.

Show time.

"I can't remember being that person," she lied, not ready to turn and face the man who'd snapped the shot when he was a yearbook staffer and not a well-known professional photographer. Not that she hadn't spent the majority of the reunion's kick-off cocktail party staring at him. While she had given the impression of listening attentively to former classmates, she'd watched Jack do the same across the room. She studied his square-jawed face, which had hardened well with age, his emerald eyes, which still glinted with an edge of mischievous daring, and his athletic physique, which fit impressively into his expensive Italian suit. Oh, she'd seen him, all right—enough to know it wouldn't be easy to go through with her plan. Enjoyable, maybe, but definitely not easy.

But she had to get Jack Sullivan out from under her skin. There had been long stretches of time when she hadn't thought of him, hadn't romanticized the short, sweet relationship they'd enjoyed. But those times were over. For the past year, he'd been increasingly a part of her life, even though he didn't know it. She had to prove to herself, once and for all, that a long-term association with the man would be bad news.

Her plan was simple—sleep with him, prove to herself how meaningless sex would be, then move on to someone who could give her the commitment she demanded.

After all, she had a daughter to protect—the child of her best friend, Chryssie, whom Angela had adopted when Chryssie died five years ago. She tried not to think about Dani now, but how could she not, with Jack standing right behind her, his ocean-green eyes, so like Dani's, staring at her?

She gathered her resolve. Jack didn't know about Dani. Maybe he never would. But she definitely wouldn't tell him until she squelched her lasting attraction to him. "That girl in the picture and I are no longer acquainted."

"Oh, come on," he contested. "You can't have changed that much since graduation, my prairie angel."

He took a step closer when he voiced the secret pet name, and his breath singed the back of her neck. Her lids fluttered. She could feel his hands just behind her— not touching her, but wanting to. Did she really want his touch again?

Then she gazed at that damned photograph. There she stood, dressed in the prairie style she'd favored then, along with every other diligent reader of *Seventeen* magazine. She looked so tellingly like a prim and proper schoolmarm from the Old West. Frills and ruffles covered her from her neck to the opaque hose tucked into calf-high boots. She'd covered up more than just skin in those days. But that was a long time ago.

Do it, Angela. You have to. Your future can't begin until you close this door to the past.

"Do I look like a prairie angel now, Jack?"

With deliberate slowness, she glanced at him over her tanned shoulder. She'd practiced the look in the mirror a hundred times. Seductive, but with a hint of coyness. Would it work?

He took a deep breath. "I've spent all evening looking for her."

"Do you really want to find her?" She kept her voice low and husky. "Or would you rather discover who I am now?"

Jack's stare met hers and matched the challenge that was ten years in the making.

"Oh, I don't know. I always liked you as a brunette," he teased, twining one of the tendrils of her dramatically upswept and newly colored auburn tresses around his finger. "And your fashion sense has changed." He glanced to where the halter top of her black crepe outfit ended, leaving her midriff bare until the material resumed at her hips and ended well above her knees. "But I wonder if you're still hiding behind your clothes."

She turned away, but only for an instant. He hadn't lost his perceptiveness, that was for sure. Now, however, she knew how to distract him.

"There's not much to hide behind anymore," she quipped, smiling as his gaze dipped to her revealing neckline.

His face was inches from hers. "A woman like you doesn't need much to hide behind."

If he'd been wrong, it wouldn't have been so difficult for her to laugh.

His proximity unnerved her, but she squared her shoulders, determined. She had to grab this opportunity before she lost her courage, before the enticing scent of his cologne and the audacious look in his eyes sent her running for safety.

Since graduation, she'd tortured herself with the question, "What if?" So he hadn't known she wore a skimpy teddy underneath her prom dress, or that she'd started on the Pill two weeks before. She'd decided to give him her virginity, but he ended up giving her grief because she'd danced with a friend instead of with him.

They'd had a shouting match, which ended with Jack stomping off and Chryssie's boyfriend agreeing to drive her home. Except for graduation and a brief encounter at a college party, she hadn't seen Jack since. She had every right to ask herself, "What if," to wonder how good it would have been.

Especially after she'd discovered the secret that propelled Jack from the back burner of her heart to the forefront of her life. Her only chance to control her future and Dani's centered on permanently destroying the indomitable bond tying Jack to her.

She stood firm and feigned indifference to his insight. "I take it, then, that your opinion of me hasn't changed. I don't know if I remember the exact words you said on prom night—"

"I said," he interrupted, "that you were cold, frigid

and repressed. I said," he emphasized, his eyes piercing her like flame-tipped arrows, "that you'd never allow yourself to fall so completely in love with someone that you'd surrender every inch of your soul."

As she heard the words again, so clearly, from a voice so familiarly throaty and cocksure, her confidence nearly faltered. "Those were awfully big words coming from a high school senior whose greatest sexual experience probably happened in the back seat of his Mustang convertible," she said, urging herself back into the character she'd assumed for the night.

The corner of his mouth flickered upward to form an arrogant grin. "Don't knock it till you've tried it."

She managed an impertinent smile as she took a step away from him. "Maybe I will."

He grabbed her hand. She willed it not to tremble.

"After all these years, you intend to try it?"

She lifted one eyebrow. "Too bad you don't still have that Mustang, or you might find out."

From behind them, the reunion chairperson's disembodied voice thanked the alumni for a great evening and ran down the list of Saturday activities at the beach resort. Some of the crowd trickled into the hotel atrium, laughing and talking, making plans for the rest of the night.

Angela and Jack stood motionless. He let her hand drop, though they were still so caught up in each other, they barely acknowledged the group of friends who stopped to invite them for a poolside catch-up session.

"Are you up for it?" she finally asked. They'd only been alone for a few moments, but she still felt overwhelmed. She needed a diversion to give her time to recoup.

"For you, I'm always up."

So much for down time. But she didn't flinch at his all-too-clear meaning, and that seemed to shock him.

"I meant the beach," she said, stepping closer, "but if you took me literally, why don't we see what we can do?"

She turned away. Jack held his breath, fighting the urge to kiss her right then and there. All night, he'd been amazed at the changes in his prairie angel, and he'd wondered how much was real and how much was an act meant to punish him for breaking her heart in high school.

When she started down the winding stairway toward the beach, he hoped for punishment—long, unending torture like what he felt as she glided down the stairs with a wanton yet nearly imperceptible swing to her hips.

He followed Angela across the poolside deck, where she stopped to wait for him at the three-foot stone wall separating the resort from the beach. Moonlight glinted off foamy waves breaking gently on the shore about fifty yards away. A touch of the silver shine caught a diamond on Angela's earring and beckoned Jack to her like a light called to a lost mariner.

Sure, Jack had let memories of Angela drift back now and then over the past decade. He hadn't had much choice. Her willful eyes and her stubborn pout flashed into his mind at the strangest times. And with growing frequency. He'd received the reunion announcement only weeks after Lily's betrayal. What better way to cleanse himself of her treachery than a trip down memory lane with his prairie angel?

He'd have written his renewed obsession off to the consequences of first love syndrome, had there been any real love involved all those years ago. But hadn't it been only lust—fire-hot, cold-sweat, prepubescent lust? It had to be. Who knew what love was back then? Who knew now? Unfortunately, the passion they'd shared had remained unfulfilled. Sweet, prudish, obstinate Angela had refused him. Though from the look of things, very little of the Angela he once knew remained. He dared to hope that somewhere, the woman he needed still existed, despite the new, sensuous packaging.

"Do you remember taking me to the beach during high school?" Leaning against the wall, she lifted her ankle to unbuckle the thin strap of one of her spiky black heels. Her slim calves flexed and shimmered. All thoughts of his needs—except a physical one—vanished.

He knelt beside her and stared intently upward, aching to touch her. "We live in Florida. We went to the beach a lot."

She slid her foot closer to him, accepting his invitation to help remove her shoes.

"Do you remember the time after the homecoming dance? We'd only been dating a few months then."

For a moment, Jack couldn't remember anything. His mind focused solely on her slim ankle and shapely calf. Before he worked the tiny buckle of the strap, he smoothed his hands over the soft silk of her hose, imagining the feel of her skin. When she nearly pulled away, but didn't, he looked up and caught her biting her bottom lip.

He undid her shoes.

She cleared her throat. "You brought me to the beach on the night after homecoming our senior year. I didn't know what you had planned, but when we left, you were furious with me."

She leaned back on her hands and smiled. The moment of hesitation was gone.

"You wouldn't get out of the car," he reminded her.

"I didn't want sand in my hose."

"What about now?"

She slid her hands down, then under her skirt and closed her fingers around shiny black garter snaps.

"I can still think of better things to have in my hose."

Jack's mouth went dry. "So can I."

In the uncertain light, he thought he saw her hands shaking. Did she want him as much as he wanted her? As much as he'd always wanted her? He'd suspected so since he first spied her staring at him from across the room. She'd dressed as provocatively as the fashion models he photographed. She'd watched him with a bold curiosity that questioned and promised at the same time. Every signal, right down to her naughty lingerie, conveyed seductive intentions. It crossed his mind that she'd come to the reunion specifically to have him, though he tried to muster enough humility to keep his desire at bay.

This is Angela Harris. The one girl who had the good sense to keep you out of her panties. But when she took his hands and guided them to her garters, he knew what she wanted from him. The tightening in his groin increased.

She leaned forward and traced his ear with tiny, gentle strokes. "Now you have the idea."

He unsnapped one garter. Her skin, warm and humid like the night, quivered as he slid his hand around to undo its mate. Again, Angela's teeth took hold of her lower lip. He stopped, resting his hand against the supple flesh of her bottom. As much as he wanted her—as much as she acted as if she wanted him—he had to know.

"Angela, why now?"

Her expression grew serious as she trailed a soft-tipped finger around his jaw and down his neck, stopping at the pulsating throb in his throat.

"Why not now? Don't you want me? You spent the better part of our senior year trying lure me into bed. You tried every trick in the book."

"But you never gave in."

She unfastened the other set of garters herself and smiled. "Maybe your tricks weren't good enough."

He rolled down her hose with the palms of his hands, trailing the descending path with his fingers. Her spicy perfume intensified as if she'd spritzed her lingerie with the exotic scent. He couldn't fight the urge to lean forward to inhale more of the heady aroma, a mixture of cinnamon, vanilla and woman.

Every curve of her leg, every inch of her skin felt pliant beneath his touch. She slid her leg closer to him. As he slipped the filmy material off her foot, a barely audible moan escaped her lips.

He stood, grabbing both her arms with a roughness he hadn't intended. He lifted her, placing her on the wall so he could see her more clearly. "Then why now, Angela? We haven't seen each other since college. What's changed?"

Her eyes widened at his harshness, then softened as her hazel irises caught a glint of triumph. "I have, Jack. I'm a new person. Maybe I'm here to see if you are, too."

"I'm essentially the same, just older." Now wasn't the time to go into specifics. "But do you want the same person I was ten years ago—a juvenile gigolo who didn't have the sense to hold onto the one decent girl who ever dared to be interested in him?"

For the briefest instant, Jack glimpsed fear in her eyes. He'd hit a sensitive spot. Sure, he'd hoped Angela would be at the reunion—still single and perhaps open to rekindling the sparks she'd doused in their youth. But he'd never expected his prairie angel to have turned into a wanton temptress. Part of him reveled in the prospect. The other part mourned.

She splayed her hands on his chest, running them under his jacket until she reached his pounding heart. "If I'm not that good girl anymore, Jack, are you still interested? Or were you just playing games back then, trying to get one of the last senior class virgins into your back seat?"

She moved her face closer to his. Her breath warmed his lips.

"I played a lot of games with you, angel," he admitted.

"Then why not continue?" She punctuated her sentence with a kiss—a brief touch, barely enough to leave her scarlet lipstick on his mouth. Her eyes remained open, and he couldn't tear his gaze from hers. He could read nothing there beyond the promise of a blinding, almost wrathful passion that would ensue if they carried this further.

When he heard the crowd approaching from behind, Jack didn't know if he was frustrated or relieved. He stepped back, fighting a flash of guilt that rode on the same wave of nostalgia that had brought him home.

Angela grabbed him by his lapel and pulled him close. "I came here for you. Don't tell me you've changed so much you aren't turned on."

"I can't deny that. But maybe I have changed enough to want to know *why* you want me."

She avoided his question. "We have company."

A dozen of their classmates poured from the hotel and pulled lounge chairs around a distant corner of the pool. They tossed out beer and wine coolers and started their party again. Someone snapped on a radio but turned down the volume as the music echoed against the hotel rooms that formed a semicircle around the pool. Mike Nichols, class clown extraordinaire, waved to Angela and Jack before his wife admonishingly slapped him on the shoulder.

Jack nodded in acknowledgment, then turned his back, shielding Angela from the cluster of prying eyes.

"You didn't answer my question, angel. Why now?"

Her gaze darted from his, then quickly returned. Again, the hesitation. It was almost as if she was persuading herself to go through with her seduction.

Before he called her on it, she spoke. "When we were in high school, you all but begged me to sleep with you. I don't think you ever realized saying no wasn't easy for me."

"But you did. Many times."

She looked down. Her dark lashes formed a delicate fan on her fair skin. When she looked up, the flecks of green in her hazel irises intensified, made glossy by moisture forming around them. "Then just when I decided to say yes, you didn't ask."

He braced himself by widening his stance. "What are you talking about?"

"Do the words 'prom night' mean anything to you?"

Her words hit him like a blow to the gut. He would have backed away again, but she still held fast to his lapels. Her melancholy expression changed suddenly to bitter anger. Fists clenched his jacket.

"I wanted to give you the most special present I could

think of, Jack, but you left me on the dance floor before
I had a chance. Do you know how that made me feel?"

The words tumbled out, deliberately quiet yet painfully loud as his brain spun in a time warp to the night
in question. He shook his head. Contrary to what she
probably believed, Jack remembered their prom as viv-
idly as she did, though for entirely different reasons. He
had every excuse to forget that night, but not because of
Angela. They'd had a fight. He'd called her those awful
names. They'd broken up. It was what happened after
his departure that he wanted to erase.

"I had no idea." He met her gaze with all the sincerity
he possessed. The regret he'd harbored all these years
escalated like a class-one hurricane hitting the Gulf
Stream. How could he have been so blind? Girls like
Angela didn't make decisions to sleep with their boy-
friends lightly. There must have been clues—clues he
stupidly ignored—and he hurt her in the process. "I
swear to you."

Her mood quickly changed again, back to the seductive sprite who'd tempted him so deliciously all night.
Her smile was slight, her eyes narrowed. "Of course
you didn't. We got into some silly fight before I had a
chance to show you how I felt. Richard Lassiter took me
home after he and Chryssie had one of their usual
knock-down-and-drag-outs. We were a pretty pathetic
couple, he and I. I was even home before midnight."

Jack mulled over her confession, then thought about
the last ten years. How would his life have been different if he had known? What about hers? Was it too late to
find out?

"But that's the past, Jack." She tugged him a little
closer. "I made up my mind a few years ago that I was
going to find out what I'd missed. Any objections?"

This time her kiss was more demanding, immediately bringing Jack to the present. Her lips were warm and open to him, and she tasted like sweet brandy. Her tongue didn't wait for his conquest, but began one of its own. Only moments passed before he remembered their rhythm, how she always tilted her head to the right, how she slid her arms under his and molded herself to his chest.

Then he thought of the heat he'd felt when he rolled down her stockings and how strong and smooth her legs were against his wandering fingers. He longed to explore the rest of her. Were her breasts still as round and inviting as they'd been when they were forbidden? Did she still have that crescent moon birthmark on the small of her back?

Would she still moan when he crooked his finger under her chin and then bathed her face in featherlight kisses?

The pressure of his need grew fierce. He ached to carry her to the beach, lay her on the sand and discover the depths of her passion. He'd come home searching for his lost innocence. He'd come in search of Angela. Now he'd found her, wrapped in provocative clothing and speaking with bold innuendo. And yet, brief hesitations and quivering hands hinted his angel hadn't changed as much as she wanted him to believe.

She broke the kiss, panting slightly. She grabbed the handkerchief from his coat pocket, then dipped the dark cloth into the moisture that had gathered between her breasts.

"I'm hot out here, aren't you?" She took the corner of the linen and smoothed away the lipstick stains from his mouth.

"Is that a trick question?" He could barely breathe.

His tie choked him like a hemp noose, and sweat trick-led down his back, pasting his shirt to scorched skin. Yet he knew the fire fevering him couldn't be cooled with water or ice. He needed Angela to douse this flame as only a woman could.

As only *this* woman could.

"It's always cooler near the water," she suggested, sliding off the concrete wall and taking the two small steps to the low gate leading to the beach. Her hands furrowed into a stack of oversize towels left by the re-sort staff for patrons taking late-night swims. "Want to take a dip?"

"Swimming in the gulf at night is dangerous." She'd lived in the state all her life. She knew the perils as well as he did, maybe better.

But the fiery glint in her eyes verified a secret wish.

The danger turned her on. *He* turned her on.

"You'll protect me, won't you, Jack?"

She lifted two fluffy towels, hugged them to her chest and started toward the shore.

For a tortuous moment, Jack watched Angela disap-pear down the driftwood walkway, past the reach of the dimmed resort lights into the inky blackness of beach and surf. The clouded sky and slivered moon muted her form like a mist, surrounding her like an ethereal creature of fantasy and dream.

Had he the patience, he would have marveled longer at the irony. He'd come to the reunion to rediscover the lost innocence of his youth—an ideal fairy tale conjured by his jaded soul. Instead, he found Angela trans-formed into a siren, capable of seducing his soul away from him.

But his patience ran out a long time ago. A decade ago, to be exact. With a cursory thought to the condom in his wallet and the crowd around the pool, he slipped off his loafers, tossed them beside Angela's abandoned strappy heels and followed the path her bare feet left in the sand.

She stood beside the darkened pier, the towels spread at the shore's edge, her bare back glistening in the moonlight. Questions flew through his brain like shooting stars—each blazing, yet too quick for a mind befuddled by raw desire.

Except one.

"What do you want, angel?"

He placed a downy kiss just below her ear, then lower, feathering warmth along the base of her neck. She cooed and hugged herself, torn between languishing in the tingly sensation shooting through her body and fighting the overwhelming need to run away. Smoothing strong hands down her arms, he worked them free, then maneuvered her in a half circle until she faced him.

"Tell me what you want," he insisted again.

Lord, didn't he know? Couldn't he feel her heart hammering against her ribs? Couldn't he sense the quivering of her skin? Didn't he realize that if he released his arms from around her, she'd probably fall to the sand like a castaway shell?

"I want you."

A grin shaped his lips and lightened his eyes. "How do you want me? Do you want me here? Now? In the water or on the towels? Clothed or naked?"

She shook her head as emphatically as she could while he renewed his attention to her neck. She tugged at his lapels, removed his jacket and tossed it to the ground. "I don't know. I don't care."

He stepped back. "You have to care, angel. I want

you to know exactly how you want me before I proceed."

She eyed him warily, then felt a wicked smile spread on her face. "You're teasing me. You're drawing this out."

"Ten years have passed since I last tried to seduce you." His forehead creased slightly, betraying the gravity of his words. "This is already drawn out. Tell me what you want."

Her gaze focused on the towels she'd tossed to the sand. They reminded her of the countless times he'd tried to make love to her in high school only to be thwarted by her fears. She wasn't about to make that mistake again. It had cost her ten years of wondering what she'd missed.

"I want tonight to be like prom night would have been."

His smile was lopsided. "I was pretty clumsy back then."

She shook her head. "Feel free to add any improvements in your technique."

He slipped his hands into his pockets, a smile glittering in his eyes.

"What's so funny?" she asked, unable to suppress an uncomfortable giggle.

"This." Again, the memory of the innocence he'd long since lost came crashing at him like a wave in a storm. His palms were sweaty, and his heart raced double time. Only Angela could do this to him. Only Angela could fill him with that delicious uncertainty that made every moment an adventure and every instant a discovery.

"I feel like I should check my watch to make sure I get you home before curfew."

She slid her hands up his chest and clasped them around his neck. "We've got all night, Jack." Kissing the tip of his chin, she combed her hands into his hair. "Make love to me, Jack. We've waited long enough."

2

RELUCTANTLY, Jack unhooked Angela's arms from around his neck and guided them to her sides. He tugged off his tie, then opened the top button of his shirt.

She stood nearly motionless, her only movement the capture of her bottom lip between her teeth.

"You're willing to surrender your soul to me, angel?"

Her voice wavered. "Maybe just a little piece. For a little while."

"I want more." He leaned forward and kissed her left temple, inhaling the subtle scent of her perfume—a familiar fragrance that reminded him of football games and video arcades. "I won't hurt you."

But he had once. Tonight gave him the chance to undo all the wrongs he'd pressed on the one woman who deserved nothing but tenderness. As sophisticated and elegant as she looked this evening, her eyes betrayed the shadow of the innocent, naive girl she'd once been—the girl he needed to save his battered soul.

She swallowed deeply then reached behind her to undo her halter top.

He took her hands in his and kissed her knuckles. "Let me do that. I would have, back then."

"Would have what?"

He encircled her waist with open hands. "I would have taken this off...slowly. I would have savored every kiss, every touch, every peeling away of clothing."

Her left eyebrow lifted skeptically. "You think so?"

"I would've tried. For you, angel, I would've tried."

His lips pressed against hers, softly at first, ensnaring her with a ribbon of blissful comfort that caused her muscles to relax from the top of her shoulders to the ends of her toes. She didn't trust him, really—she couldn't, after all she knew about him. Yet in this, she felt safe. He couldn't hurt her. To hurt her, she'd have to really care about him, like she thought she had before.

But she didn't anymore. She wouldn't. She couldn't.

She parted her lips and allowed his tongue to slip inside. His hands did no more than knead her waist and hips, but the fire between them needed little kindling. She pressed against his full, muscled length and dug her fingers into his skin.

Their kiss grew ravenous when his hands dipped to cup her bottom. She was flooded with the delicious thrill that once accompanied such a simple indulgence—and still did. Her skin prickled with a wicked warmth.

His lips left hers to trail once again to her neck, where he suckled her pulse points and nipped at her ear. She leaned her head back, moaning as his deft hands undid the hooks of her halter top, untied the back, then slid down to undo the zipper on her skirt. With a gentle tug, the crepe fell to her ankles, leaving her in nothing but panties and garter belt, the straps dangling and tickling her bare thighs.

Silently, she unbuttoned the rest of his shirt, pulling the crisp material away from his broad chest and over his muscled shoulders as slowly as she could. She ran her hands down his chest, watching her fingers mingle in the curled chest hair, feeling the taut sinews beneath his skin, wondering if she would have had the confidence to appreciate such male beauty before.

"Did I ever touch you like this?" She undid his belt and zipper, then splayed her fingers around his tapered waist, dipping into the waistband of his briefs.

His heavy eyelids and slightly opened mouth gave her the answer she sought.

"What a fool I was," she murmured.

He grabbed her elbows just as his pants fell to the ground. "You weren't a fool, angel. You were wise to stay away from me. To keep me away." He pulled her to him, so close she could see the darkened pupils of his eyes. "I wouldn't have gone slow. I would've fumbled and groped, and it would've all been over in a New York minute. But not now, angel. Not tonight."

He wrapped one arm around her and lifted her with the grace of a dancer.

"Tonight—" he punctuated his promise with a kiss on the tip of her nose "—I'm going to make up for the ten years we could have had."

Spoken with such assurance, his pledge nearly rocked her resolve. If she'd made love to him then, would they still be together now? Impossible. They'd been children, teenagers with little in common except an interest in journalism and unrequited lust. Consummating that lust would only have ended their dalliance sooner, as it would now.

Wouldn't it?

His lips banished the question from her mind, intoxicated her with his taste, his scent. His muscled arms held her tight and secure against any residual fear or doubt. Even when she heard his feet splash into the water and felt the tepid gulf water rising around them, she thought of nothing but taking his body into hers.

When the water reached his waist, he lowered himself to his knees, immersing Angela to the tips of her breasts. The entwined sensations of warm water, cool night air and Jack made her nipples pucker and darken. When he turned her and guided her legs around his waist, she moaned. He was thick and long and ready. But the sound of her need died against the pressure of his lips and tongue. Her flesh thrummed. Her blood pounded. The lapping of the water against the pier faded beneath the allegro cadence of her heart.

They kissed for what seemed like forever. Finally, they broke, gasping as if they'd been submerged. He lifted her higher and gazed at her hungrily.

"You are still so gorgeous." He placed a surprisingly sweet kiss in the valley between her breasts, then nuzzled his nose against her moist skin. "How could I have ever..."

His sentiment died on his lips, lips he used instead to bath her in langorous kisses. His hands on her rib cage, he lifted her breasts, flicking her nipples alternately with tongue and thumb pad until she threw back her head and murmured his name.

He eased her down, thrusting his sex against hers, using the friction of flesh and saturated material to intensify the sensations ravaging her body. He kissed her hard, with precision, as if he took in every measure of her mouth with his tongue and her body with his hands.

"Oh, Jack," she cried, not knowing when, if ever, she'd felt so trapped and so free at the same time. Jack held a portion of her heart like a sparrow in a cage. Only his touch could free her—and send her soaring. She reached into the water, grasped the edge of his briefs and tugged.

"Not yet, angel. Hold on."

She shook her head, dizzy with desire, weakened by need.

"Just a minute more. Heaven's just a minute away." He caressed her buttocks and hips, kissed her shoulders, slid a wet hand up her spine, bracing her as he carried her from the water and placed her on the thick towels she'd draped along the shore.

The pier acted as a shadow canopy, the moon a dim candle just bright enough to be caught by beads of water sliding down Jack's chest, over his flat stomach, curling the hair on his powerful thighs. He lay alongside her, warming her with his heat, kissing her with lips that tasted of wine and salt water.

He slipped out of his briefs, then ripped her panties away with barely an effort. He tugged at the dangling straps of the garter belt he'd left draped around her hips until she pressed fully against him.

"Do you still want this, angel?"

He spoke the question with his mouth hovering near hers. His breath made her quiver. His hands slid between them.

"Jack, I..." She lost her voice when he dipped a finger inside her.

"You're so wet. And not from the water. From me. You're wet because you want me."

She knew what he sought, as strongly as she knew what she wanted from him. He needed her to tell him. In words. Again.

"Yes, Jack, I want you. I've always wanted you. I can't breathe right now from wanting you."

Her breasts yearned for his touch. Her neck implored

for his kiss. She needed him all over her, inside her, penetrating every boundary until he filled her with the force of his passion.

For the briefest moment he left her, but after she heard the jingle of his belt and a tear of foil, he rolled and made up for lost time with deep, long kisses down her neck.

He straddled her, and she dug her nails into his shoulders, through his damp hair and across his back, nearly bucking when his mouth sought her nipple with a powerful tug. She arched against him, tossing her head from side to side. The edge was too close. She couldn't slip over without him.

"I've waited ten years, angel. I can't wait a minute more."

"Then don't."

She wrapped her legs around him possessively, gasping at the sensation of his tip against her throbbing folds. She fought to swallow. He lifted her hips, stroked her with his hand and sex until she opened her mouth to scream. Just then, he entered and kissed away her cry.

His eyes widened in amazed pleasure. "You're so tight. Oh, angel, I didn't..."

She clutched his buttocks. "Love me, Jack."

With his thrust, she yelped, at once shocked and enraptured by the pleasure-pain of their joining. He rested within her, taking her mouth completely, kissing her thoroughly until her body adjusted. Soon she moved beneath him, tilting upward to fully accept him inside her.

"Move with me, angel." Jack braced himself above her on one arm, allowing the other hand to tend to her breast. "You're so sweet and tight. Ooh, angel."

His words were like a litany, a song of adoration that made her soar. "Yes, Jack, yes." The words tumbled from her lips, urging him on.

The first orgasm ripped straight through her. She shuddered and shivered as ecstasy transfused through her veins.

"Oh, Jack." She gripped his shoulders, pulling him forward until his body draped hers.

"We're not done." He slowed his pace, but continued to move inside her.

"But, I..." She protested, sure there couldn't be any more—at least, not for her.

"Not good enough." He nuzzled her neck and flipped her over so she lay on top of him.

"I can't."

He clutched her hips. "Yes, you can. And you will."

Still rigid and muscled, he eased into her. The new sensation brought her bolt upright. Movement came as naturally as breathing.

"That's it. You're so beautiful. So amazing."

He kept one hand on her hip, holding her, encouraging her to accept the overwhelming feel of him joined with her and under her control. With his other hand, he caressed her breasts, cupping her flesh lovingly, grazing her nipples with his thumb.

She brought her knees under her and braced her hands on his chest. Arching, she accepted the fullness of him, raising and lowering herself until he grabbed her hips with both hands and rocked into her with the urgency of a desperate man.

He cried out her name when he came, and she accompanied him over the boundary and into the chasm of delirious pleasure. She fell forward, rasping but sated, against his moisture-slickened chest. After a brief, still moment, he wrapped his arms around her, enfolding her in a cocoon of warmth.

When his breathing slowed, he rolled over, pinning her beneath him. The look in his eyes was a mixture of delight and confusion.

"This was your first time in a while, wasn't it?"

She swallowed the irrational tears building behind her eyes. Her first, and last, sexual relationship had been almost nine years ago. "Was I that inexperienced?"

"Inexperienced?" His voice lilted with carefully controlled laughter. He stroked her cheek lovingly, soothing away her fear. "You made me feel things I've never felt before. It's just that you were so tight. I can't believe..."

She finally mustered the conviction to look at him squarely. "You can't believe that I don't hop in and out of bed with dozens of men on a regular basis?"

He shook his head, then kissed her sweetly on the cheek. "I can't believe I deserved such a rare and special gift."

For the briefest instant, in the tilt of her smile, Jack spied the innocence he'd missed all night. Despite the smudged red lipstick, dark-lined eyes and wanton lovemaking, the naiveté was still there in his prairie angel.

In the distance, Jack could hear that the crowd at the pool had increased. He reached for his jacket, draping it modestly over her, just in case. No doubt the gossip had raged when they left the pool. They had once been an item—an unlikely pair, but a couple nonetheless. How unusual could it be for high school sweethearts to get back together after a decade apart?

Of course, Jack reminded himself, they hadn't had a

reconciliation. Just sex. Great sex. Unbelievably great sex.

Sex that might lead to something more, if he played his cards right.

"I think we should get dressed."

Her eyebrow tilted upward. "Afraid we'll get caught?" she asked. "My sister's not here to ground me, Jack."

Despite her lighthearted ribbing, Jack didn't laugh. He had just made a decision, a choice he hadn't believed he'd ever make. Not after his fiasco with Lily.

But Lily wasn't Angela. None of the women he'd wasted his time with measured up even remotely to her. He'd come to the reunion to seek his lost innocence. He'd come to find Angela. He'd be damned if he let her go now.

"This isn't over, Angela. Not by a long shot."

She motioned for her clothes. "You seem awfully sure of yourself. How do you know I didn't want just a one-night stand? You remember those, don't you?"

He flinched, wondering how much she knew about his past and the regrets he'd logged since prom night his senior year. But that conversation was a long way away, especially if he wanted Angela to remain in his life past the weekend. He put his pants on, neglecting his briefs, and stuffed her panties into his pocket. She'd slipped on her skirt but needed help tying the top of her halter. He worked carefully, not trusting himself to touch her again so soon.

He spoke straight into her ear, willing himself not to falter under the fragrance of her perfume. "Tonight was unbelievable, angel. I want you. I'm not touching you, but I can feel you all over me. I'm not kissing you, but the sweet taste of you is still in my mouth."

"So, should we call this an appetizer?"

He shook his head, wondering at the challenge she posed. "The first course. And I intend to partake of the whole meal."

"Hungry again?"

"Famished." He pulled on his shirt and straightened his jacket. "But tonight, I've had a healthy portion. I'd like to know more about the menu before I dig in again."

She shrugged, then extended her hand so he could help her up. He did, but she didn't immediately let go.

Looking into his eyes, she studied him. He could see the questions in her expression, and the surrender, as well.

"Okay, Jack. I appreciate whetting the appetite. I just hope when you're ready, I'll still be in the mood for the full five-course meal."

He smiled wickedly and led her toward the resort. "*Seven* courses. And if you aren't, it'll be my turn to entice your palate."

She smirked at him before swinging past him with that seductive little walk of hers. She stopped not two steps away, grabbed her shoes and threw a coy glance over her shoulder.

"Can we extend a metaphor, or what?"

With that, she was gone, waving demurely at her classmates, who grew instantly quiet as she passed.

If he didn't know that the pool water was a sultry eighty degrees, he would have jumped right in.

EXHAUSTED, Angela showered away the sticky salt water, scrubbed off her makeup, changed into her pajamas and climbed into bed. She flew through the nightly ritual as quickly as possible, trying not to think, willing herself not to analyze what had happened on the beach. But with the lights off and her body encased in a silk negligee instead of her familiar knee-length nightshirt and floppy socks, she couldn't help feeling ridiculous.

Embarrassed.

Thrilled.

What had she been thinking? Making love to Jack had been marvelous—as wonderful as she'd imagined, even slightly better. But it wasn't over. It couldn't be. She'd had a taste and she wouldn't be able to resist another bite.

How would that fit into her plan?

In the past decade, her life had been nothing like what she'd planned. Normalcy was nonexistent. Even her successes had a bittersweet flavor. She'd finished college a year early. Her internship at Waynscot International, a fledgling marketing firm, turned into a full-time position just before the company found a niche and market shares soared sky-high. She was twenty-one and making more money than she'd ever imagined.

Then she'd gotten the call from California.

Chryssie, her best friend, was dead, and Angela had become a single mother. Her life would never be the same.

After pounding her pillow with her fist, she finally settled down. That was all old news. She'd adjusted to the changes tragedy had imposed on her, and in the four years that followed, she'd started her own marketing firm, researching companies, gauging the gaps between the product and consumer and creating business plans to close the separation with cutting-edge promotions and advertising.

Then, a year ago, she'd gotten news that would drag

her back into a relationship with the man who'd broken her heart.

Suddenly, the silky smoothness of her short nightgown didn't seem so foreign or uncomfortable. Despite a few moments of uncertainty, she'd slipped easily into the role of seductress. With Jack around, it wasn't difficult. The man could melt ice with a glance.

She hadn't known much about her sexuality. She'd had neither the time nor the inclination to explore that aspect of her life beyond one college fling. After Jack's rejection, she'd searched for someone to share her bed. Sex became something to do—an act more expected than anticipated. Disappointed with her one and only experience, she'd focused on her career.

But tonight proved that ten years was more than worth the wait. She relished the residual ache of their lovemaking. She languished in the memory of his touch. The sensation of his weight lingered on her. The scent of his cologne clung to her like the silk of her negligee.

She'd only sampled a tidbit of pleasure at his hands, and she couldn't deny his power. For a moment, she'd almost lost herself in the emotions of the experience. Only the last vestiges of anger had kept her in control. She'd come so close to releasing some of the resentment. But to what end?

She'd come to the reunion to put the lingering fantasies to rest. That's all. Jack Sullivan might be a delicious lover, but he'd never make a faithful husband.

Or father.

Her heart still cried when she remembered the day she brought Dani home. The four-year-old orphan, so scared and unsure, clutched her worn rag doll, afraid to stay alone for more than a minute, terrified Angela would disappear like her mother had. Over a year passed before Dani reverted to the free-spirited child she'd once been—and still was. With her love for the child as her guide, Angela had managed to create a secure family for her and Dani, one she wouldn't disrupt for anyone—not even Jack Sullivan.

If she let out all the stops, nature would take its course. She and Jack would have their affair and then she'd be through with him. "What if?" would be answered, and she could go on with her life.

How hard could leaving him be?

AS SOON AS SHE switched off the faucet and shook her toothbrush, a knock on the door sent Angela scrambling for her robe. Room service sure worked quick around here.

"Hold on a minute." She tugged her sash into a semblance of a knot. "Who is it?"

"Your breakfast, madam," answered a muffled voice.

Raising herself on tiptoe to see out the ridiculously high peephole, she spied a large covered tray. And little else.

Cautiously, she opened the door.

"Good morning, angel."

Jack lowered the tray, dazzling her with a smile that rivaled the morning sun. Dressed in a loose-fitting gray tank top and black shorts, he looked ready to hit the mild surf.

She tore her gaze from the sleek lines of his triceps bulging beneath the weight of the tray, but not before he caught her looking.

Sarcasm covered her embarrassment. "I should have guessed you'd show up, begging for a meal, first thing this morning." She leaned cockily against the door.

"Don't get too excited, sweetheart. The kind of hunger I'm entertaining this morning is strictly culinary. I just thought you might want to talk over a cup of sobering coffee."

She swung the door open in invitation. "Sobering? I wasn't drunk last night. Maybe I should have been. Then I'd have an excuse."

With his back to her as he cleared a table near the balcony, Jack didn't suppress a knowing grin. There she was, his saber-toothed angel.

"I just knew you weren't all willingness and sex appeal." He uncovered steaming plates of eggs Benedict, fresh melon and croissants for two. "As I recall, your sharp tongue got you several stays in the vice-principal's office."

She pulled back the curtains and opened the balcony door, surprised at the uncommonly cool morning breeze. She scanned the sky for signs of rain. Several dark clouds loomed in the west, but the rest of the sky was newly washed with the bright marmalade hues of morning.

"My sharp tongue often comes in handy."

She turned to find him sitting at the table, popping pieces of croissant into his mouth like peanuts. He leaned back leisurely, as if he was paying the one-hundred-and-fifty-dollar-a-night rent on her suite. Not that he couldn't afford it. She wouldn't be surprised if he'd taken the penthouse down the hall. Being a world-class photographer brought in world-class fees.

"Comfortable?" she asked.

"I'd be more comfortable if you'd join me. Your eggs are getting cold."

He stood and pulled out a chair for her. She couldn't resist. In her nervousness last night, she hadn't managed more than a few nibbles of dinner. This morning, she was famished. Besides, in the daylight, Jack looked more like an old friend and less like a conquest—despite a devastating smile that went from his curved lips to his ocean-green eyes.

After a sip of orange juice and a bite of egg, she caught him watching her over his coffee.

"Thanks for breakfast," she said.

"You're welcome. But I have to be honest—I have ulterior motives."

Angela laughed as she balanced a piece of egg on her fork. "I expected as much, though I didn't think you'd admit it so blatantly. Maybe you have changed."

"Maybe I have."

His serious tone brought her gaze up, but he wasn't looking in her direction. Jack's stare extended to the distant horizon. The sky, painted by the newborn sun, still reflected a few streaks of pink, orange and purple. It was beautiful, but not unusual for Florida. The scenery hadn't taken his focus away. A faraway thought had.

"Care to tell me how?"

The question was out before she could stop it. Did she really want to know if Jack had changed? What if his answer upset her plans?

He grinned and leaned forward to sample his breakfast. "I might. If you agree to reciprocate."

"My life story for yours?"

"Just the last ten years. I think I have a handle on the eighteen before."

Angela poured herself a cup of coffee, then added cream and sugar. "It's been a long time. Do you really expect me to believe you remember my past?"

"Contrary to your memories of me, angel, I did care about you. I listened when you talked. I remember when your father died in our sophomore year. I remember going with you to your sister's wedding the February before we graduated. How are Kelly and her husband? What was his name?"

Feeling slightly chagrined and knowing full well from his expression that he knew what her brother-in-law's name was, she jabbed at a strip of bacon. "His name was and is Garrett. They're still married and they have two kids, ages twelve and eight. My mom travels around a lot with the business, just like she and Dad used to. We see her about four times a year, a couple of weeks at a time."

"We?" Jack probed.

Angela just managed to avoid choking as she swallowed, then grabbed her juice. "Me and Kelly. The family. They live next door."

Good recovery.

"What about your mother?" she asked quickly before she nearly blew it again, "Is she still married to Paul?"

Jack took a swig of coffee. "I'm afraid Paul bit the dust about four years ago. She's with a man named Sam or Steve, last time I checked, anyway."

Angela dropped the subject. Obviously, his resentment over his mother's multiple husbands hadn't receded.

"So, where are you living now?"

Over the rest of breakfast, they filled each other in on the more innocuous portions of their lives. Jack told her about his new studio, a renovated warehouse in Ybor City, the historical Latin district east of Tampa. She explained how companies hired her marketing firm to determine strategies for connecting target consumers with their products. They talked about his travels all over the world as a photographer and the recurring bouts of jet lag that eventually brought him home. She talked more about her sister, brother-in-law and nephews, careful not to mention Dani.

His daughter.

"What about your personal life, Angela? You haven't said much about that."

"Neither have you."

"Oh, come on," he said with a skeptical attempt at surprise. "Don't tell me you didn't pick up the tabloids when no one was looking. My face was plastered on them for two solid weeks."

"I didn't need to," she answered. "Tampa isn't that big. Gossip gets around."

"I'm sure it does," he muttered derisively before sitting back and hooking his hands behind his head. "Let's see, my love life, in a nutshell. Relatively uneventful until recently. Beautiful women, beautiful places, one beautiful model, ugly results. Any questions?"

She piled the empty plates on top of each other. "It wasn't my question in the first place."

He saluted her with his orange juice. "True. But since you've chosen a life-style that keeps you out of the professional gossip trade, you'll have to tell me on your own."

"There isn't much to tell."

Standing, Angela picked up her coffee and moved onto the balcony. Though the July breeze had a cool hint of impending rain, she felt stifled and hot. She couldn't discuss that aspect of her life with him, no matter how much her heart told her she should.

"Touchy subject?" he asked as he joined her.

She shrugged. "Not at all. I just think we've acted

normal enough this morning. We've evaded the one topic that seemed uppermost to us last night."

With that, she caught sight of her reflection in the sliding glass door. She'd barely had time to finish her morning ritual before he came knocking. Though she'd showered, washed her face and brushed her teeth, she still hadn't straightened her hair or put on makeup. She looked more like she did on an average day at home than in the middle of a carefully planned weekend of seduction.

But she didn't have time to go inside for a quick fix before Jack swooped and pulled her into a deep, lingering kiss. His hands circled her waist, demandingly molding her to him. Her breasts were crushed against his hard chest. Through the delicate material of her robe, she could feel every taut muscle.

Her response was immediate and jolting—an electric shock of passion. Every nerve snapped to attention. Every inch of her skin tingled. His power sapped her breath, and when she tried to replenish her lungs, she inhaled the overwhelming scents of bay spice and gulf breeze.

"Is this the topic you meant?" he whispered into the hollow of her neck. He looked into her eyes, and she lost herself in the ocean-green depths of his irises. With his finger, he traced the planes of her face, then crooked his knuckle under her chin, holding her steady while he bathed her face in downy kisses.

She moaned.

He grinned.

Her mind swirled with conflicting signals. She knew she should be in control, but she couldn't clear her head. She didn't really want to. Thinking logically caused her to lose Jack the first time. Over and over,

she'd told herself that to seduce Jack, she'd have to surrender to the storm of emotions and physical responses
he would stir. She'd thought she could handle that. But
now she felt as if she was in the eye of the very storm
she'd steered toward. Fear scurried up her spine like a
sailor up a mast.

"You're trembling," he pointed out between kisses.

"Congratulations," she rasped.

He stopped his assault. "I don't want you to be
afraid."

She couldn't pass up the perfect chance for momentary escape. Slipping by him, she searched for the hap-
hazard pins that still held her hair in a wild cascade of
curls.

"I'm not afraid of you." She stepped to the bureau
and rummaged through her handbag for a brush.

He was behind her, rubbing his palms up her silky
sleeves to massage her shoulders and neck.

"I didn't say it was me you were afraid of."

She pulled at her bangs with her brush. "Who then?
Our classmates? I thought I proved last night that I
didn't give a damn for their opinions anymore."

With his thumbs, he traced her spine, marking every
inch or so with a kiss to the back of her neck.

"Not them, either."

She stiffened and stared into the mirror to await his
attention. Yet for a tortuous minute, he continued his
hands-on study of her waist and hips. Then he looked
over her shoulder and met her gaze.

"You, my dear, are afraid of you."

3

SHE SWUNG AROUND, trapped with her backside pressed against the bureau. Jack leaned forward, diminishing all space between them. The sensation of his growing hardness against her stomach shot to her weakening knees. If he hadn't been standing so close, she feared she'd fall.

But his words rang clear.

You, my dear, are afraid of you.

"Care to explain?"

He plied the brush from her tight grasp and led her to the edge of the bed. He sat, turned her so she faced the mirror, and pulled her into the triangle between his legs. He tossed the brush aside and smoothed his hands through her hair, flinging pins away as he found them, releasing her curls until they tumbled en masse to the lower ends of her shoulder blades. He reclaimed the brush and with practiced care freed her hair of tangles.

The gentle tugs and soothing strokes lulled her to silence. He eased each pull with his fingers, working slowly.

He lifted her hair from her nape.

"So soft."

His breath stirred the tiny hairs along the base of her neck, sending her skin into a thrilling prickle that spread like wildfire. Never had a man performed such a personal task in such a tantalizing way. Every stroke fired her. She'd never considered the intimacy. She spent nearly every morning brushing Dani's...

"Jack," she protested, trying to stand when her daughter's name popped into her head.

He didn't let go, but tightened his thighs around hers. "Relax, angel."

Relax. Easier said than done. She couldn't afford to think of Dani, not in the same room with the one man who could never learn of her child's existence.

She forced the name out of her mind and concentrated on the feel of the brush gliding through her hair, reviving the original wavy texture. Soon he discarded the brush and used his hands, kneading her scalp and massaging her temples.

She forgot his comment regarding her fears—forgot all about Dani and the secrets she personified. No thoughts entered Angela's mind. Only sensations. Jack's gentle yet sinewy fingers traced her ears, caressed the base of her neck, lightly dug into the juncture at her shoulders.

"Do you want me right now as much as I want you?" he murmured, burying his nose in her hair.

"Now who's asking the trick questions?"

He moved his hands, fanning them over her lap as far to her knees as he could reach, then dragged them back, dipping into the space where her robe fell open. He stroked the sensitive skin of her inner thighs and trailed his thumbs up her pelvis to her hips. He designed a swirling pattern on her skin that matched the responses building inside her.

He hardened against her backside. His skin grew feverish, and the heat seeped though his cotton tank top and her thin robe, searing her skin.

"No tricks, angel. Just conditions."

The tips of his fingers lingered along the lacy edges of her panties. She ached for him to pass under the delicate barrier and soothe the escalating ache.

Instead, he guided her across the bed, amid the rumpled sheets from her restless night, until she lay beside him. He drew her into a languid kiss, then awaited her answer.

She swallowed and fought to remember the question. "What conditions?"

He undid the already loosened tie on her robe and opened it. Except for high-cut panties, she wore nothing underneath. Involuntarily, she drew one leg up. He gently pressed it down. His gaze swept the length of her.

"You are exquisite," he said, his voice rich with need.

He traced a lazy pattern from the base of her neck to her left breast. He moistened his finger in his mouth, then grazed her nipple. The nubbin puckered instantly. She labored to breathe. Closing her eyes, she forced herself to think.

"What conditions, Jack?"

He continued his exploration around her belly button, across the outside of her right hip, then inward until his fingers disappeared beneath floral material and into the dark curls at the base of her thighs. She sucked in a breath. A quarter inch more, maybe less, and she'd explode.

He stopped. "My conditions are simple. I've had many women in my bed. Too many, if hindsight proves correct. Every one of them gave me her body willingly. Some might have given me part of their hearts, which I summarily trampled on."

"I know that feeling."

He caught and held her gaze despite her sarcasm.

"Maybe you do. But I still want something more from you."

Removing his hand from its intimate position, Jack allowed her a second to think.

Her passion subsided, though her breasts still felt heavy when she pulled her robe closed. "So these women gave you their hearts. I did that once, too. I didn't say I'd repeat the mistake. But I am curious. What more could you want from me that those women couldn't or wouldn't give you?"

She didn't move, and neither did he, though his irises seemed to darken, like the sky outside.

"Your soul."

That was enough to send her scooting away. She tied her robe with a violent jerk, though she felt still naked. "I didn't know what you meant by those words ten years ago. Or last night. I still don't."

He laid back, pulled up a pillow and folded it under his head. "What makes you think *I* know what it means?"

Even with the tinge of arrogance, his words seemed sincere. Her momentary anger was washed away as his expression returned to the one she'd noticed as he stared toward the distant horizon. He was searching. For something crucial. But what? Did she want to know?

"Then you're proposing we figure out the meaning together."

He nodded.

She drew in a deep breath and caught the growing scent of the impending storm. *How fitting.*

"That's a pretty tall order for someone who had her heart set on a simple weekend fling." She lay on her stomach, leaned on her elbows, then smiled when he finally stopped staring at the ceiling.

"Sorry to ruin your plans," he said.

"You haven't." *Not yet.* "Who says we can't give each other what we want and then go our separate ways?"

"Because we each want something different."

She shrugged and fluffed up her pillow. "Who knows if we do or not? Seems to me neither one of us is so very sure about what we want. Except for one thing."

She leaned toward him, her lips acted like a magnet. The kiss was tentative at first, like their reunion kiss should have been—but wasn't. The stakes had gone through the roof in the last few moments, but Angela couldn't deny herself the chance to get Jack Sullivan out of her system. She'd just have to be careful—for her own sake—and Dani's.

Neither of them moved to deepen the kiss. For a long minute, the touching of their lips remained chaste and pure. Her body cooled, though not entirely. She found herself immersed in a tranquil warmth that surrounded her like the summer ocean. Thoughts of hot sex were washed away, replaced by a simple kiss.

When Jack finally touched her, he only grazed her cheek, as if afraid to do more. The artlessness of his gesture reached every part of her, including her heart. She broke away, shocked.

Jack's eyes remained closed, as if he savored the moment. When he opened them, there was no hint of triumph, no indication of lust. If she didn't know better, she would have thought she spied a bit of innocent wonder.

"Jack, I..."

He pressed his forefinger across her lips, forcing the

silence to continue until he let out a long, pent-up breath.

Suddenly, even with the balcony door open in the large suite, she felt claustrophobic. Jack had changed. He'd become more complicated. More intriguing. Or she was mature enough to recognize the complexity in someone she once believed had only one thing on his mind. She'd underestimated him—then and now. That realization made her ache with guilt.

For the first time, she considered her role in the destruction of their friendship. That's what it had been, after all. He'd acted like any teenage boy whose girlfriend wouldn't put out. In fact, he'd acted better than most. She'd read about date rape. Instead, Jack had simply let her go and found someone who'd give him what he needed. Could she fault him for finding her best friend?

She rolled off the bed, and Jack didn't move to stop her. She didn't speak. She didn't yet have the words. She shut the door to the balcony and pulled the drapes closed, plunging the room into darkness.

"I'm going to get dressed," she announced quietly.

"I'll let myself out."

She wanted to tell him not to leave, to wait and they'd go to the beach together. But she didn't. They both had a lot to think about, and they'd probably think more clearly alone.

Crossing the room quickly, she grabbed the swimsuit and cover-up she'd laid out and retreated to the solitude of the bathroom. Then she just stood there, staring at herself blankly in the mirror until she heard the padding of his steps across the floor and the click of the closing door.

Desperately, she reached for the light switch. As the blackness engulfed her, she slid down the door onto the cold tile. The momentary tenderness they'd shared overwhelmed her. The need in his eyes haunted her. As much as she'd tried to avoid the intimacy, she had caught a glimpse of the Jack Sullivan who'd once captured her heart—the Jack Sullivan who, though totally unaware of it, had made her love him so desperately she'd wanted to give him the gift of her innocence.

But she hadn't come here to rediscover love. She wanted sex only—that, and closure to an unresolved physical and emotional tie she and Dani couldn't afford. Despite their lovemaking the night before, Jack remained an unanswered question in her mind. Would the sex get better? Could it? Why was he still attracted to her after all these years?

Why did he touch her so sweetly?

Until she discovered the answers, she would never be able to move on with her life and create a loving family for her adopted daughter—one that might someday include a husband and father.

She'd never imagined that Jack might be a candidate for both roles. How could she have? Jack's past, his lifestyle reeked of meaningless conquests and frivolous pursuits. He'd traveled the world in the company of fashion models and bohemian artists who changed residences with the seasons and changed tastes with the crowd. His childhood, with a fickle mother and an absent father, hadn't been conducive to creating a man who cherished long-term bonds. He didn't believe in love. He'd told her so once, and his words were impossible to forget. No way would Jack Sullivan want to be saddled with a wife and child.

Would he?

The answer had to be no. Otherwise, the lies she lived with would tumble like a ten-ton house of cards. It didn't matter that Angela hadn't started the lies or that she'd done everything she could to uncover the truth. The truth could hurt only one person—Dani.

Angela buried her face in her hands, too exhausted to cry. She let out an extended breath and willed herself to snap out of it. *Think logically.* She was a successful businesswoman. Surely her experience in the corporate arena could help her.

In business, she'd learned to finish what she started. To leave now, to throw her things into a suitcase and disappear from Jack's life would only mean more uncertainty for her and Dani. Still, she couldn't let Jack into Dani's life. She'd dated selectively, careful to protect her child from thinking she might finally get a father only to be disappointed when the relationship didn't work out. And none of them had.

But Angela made a good single parent. Dani didn't need a father. Least of all a man like Jack.

But Angela had to see this seduction through—for herself. Every frazzled nerve ending in her body swore to one truth—no power on earth could neutralize the fierce attraction she shared with Jack except the experience of making love to him again. The feel of his touch on her skin still burned. Her nipple still puckered from his teasing. Liquid heat pooled within her at that memory.

Denying her lust for him was fruitless and unrealistic. She wanted him with an indomitable force she didn't begin to understand. She had to forget that intimate moment they'd shared before she'd run into the bathroom like the frightened schoolgirl she'd once been. The innocent wonder she'd seen in his eyes had only been a flash to the past.

He wanted to explore the depths of her soul. He

wanted to touch the essence of her being. She figured there were two paths to that destination. One passed through her heart, the other through her body. She knew where to place the roadblocks.

In two weeks, Dani returned from summer camp. Angela would give herself a deadline. By the time fourteen days were up, Angela Harris would have steered Jack Sullivan into and out of her bed. Her heart would stay off-limits.

She'd end her fascination with the past forever, even if it meant denying herself the company of the sexiest man she'd ever known.

AN HOUR AND A HALF later, Jack found Angela lounging on a beach chair, her eyes closed, her lips gently parted as if waiting for a kiss. Her shimmering blue swimsuit reflected the sunlight like a doubloon newly washed ashore. The pit of his stomach sizzled at the sight, leaving him feeling younger, freer—full of the lust for life he thought he'd lost forever.

Or was it the lust for Angela?

"Is that suit safe for athletic activities?"

Angela shielded her eyes with her hand.

"I assume you mean volleyball," she ventured wryly.

Jack squatted beside her, enjoying the way she weakened his knees with her kittenish grin. "For the moment, volleyball is the safest athletic competition for the two of us. Although, based solely on the suit, I could think of a sport less...team oriented."

She swung her slim, tanned legs off the chair and dug into her bag, then donned dark shades. "You do have a one-track mind," she said without a hint of rebuke. "I'll play, but my setups are rusty."

"Oh, I wouldn't go that far." Jack stood and extended

his hand, helping her from the chair. Her skin, slick with suntan lotion, smelled of sweet coconut and tangy pineapple. "You seem to be doing a great job with me."

She pulled her hand away and tugged on her cover-up. "I was talking about volleyball."

He started toward the hotel. "So was I."

"Liar." Her tone was slightly indignant, but intrigued. She truly had no idea how deeply she affected him. "What do you think I'm setting you up for?"

Jack laughed, though the absence of humor left a hollow sound. "Don't get your bathing suit in a bunch, angel. I didn't mean anything by that."

"No, I think you did."

With her arms crossed and her hair pulled back in a high-crowned ponytail, Angela seemed every bit the willful girl he'd once toyed with so carelessly. Now he knew better. Since last night, he'd learned that the power she held over him was deeper, more intense than he'd imagined. Their lovemaking had been as fiery as a twelve-alarm brushfire during a dry spell.

He'd had hot sex before. That wasn't what burned in his memory. It was the kiss in her room, devoid of sexual context and full of simple honesty, that had seared him to the core. How many years had passed since he'd found such awe in a mere touching of lips? Probably ten, when he'd last kissed Angela Harris in high school. Of course, he'd probably been too blind then to recognize the significance.

He couldn't help resenting the way she'd played him like a tautly strung violin the previous evening, first on the pool deck and then on the shore. This morning, he'd gone to her room to tease her, entice her and perhaps make love to her again as soon as he could, to destroy the exotic spell she'd cast. But their conversation had started off so normally, so comfortably. Even when he told her about his loveless life, the regrets didn't taste as bitter.

He shook his head. Was he putting too much stock in this liaison? Maybe Angela could renew him the way he desperately hoped. Then again, maybe she would lead him into a darker hell than the one Lily introduced him to.

"Come on, angel. Let's play some volleyball."

"First, I want to know what I'm setting you up for."

Stepping closer to her, he slid his sunglasses down his nose, then did the same to hers, using his body to block the bright sun. "What else do angels set mortal men up for? A fall. A really big fall."

Despite her move to protest, Jack grabbed her hand and yanked her into a jog till they reached the net he and the guys had set up shortly after the rain shower ended. Cooked by the July sun, the morning's gray clouds had spewed forth only a brief drenching before merging with the humid air. The top layer of sand, barely saturated, clung to their feet like snow, leaving powdery white footprints along the beach.

In minutes the teams were chosen and play began. Angela's setup skills had a bit of practice, since her brother-in-law had bought a net for the boys. She and Dani played a heck of a two-woman team against her nephews.

With Jack on the opposite side spiking balls for the other team, she felt safe enough to think of Dani and of Chryssie. Angela missed her best friend. How many times had they cut their last class to head across the bay to play volleyball? Chryssie often talked her into skipping the whole day, and they'd spend the morning on the old sponge docks in Tarpon Springs, breakfasting on baklava and trying to look like tourists instead of truant teenagers. They'd lunch at an oyster bar frequented by local businessmen, whom Chryssie would flirt with until they bought her a beer and a meal.

Angela remembered feeling strangely sophisticated when these three-piece-suited execs drew them into their conversations as if they belonged. Of course, she and Chryssie learned to hold their own. Angela theorized that the seeds of her early financial successes were rooted in the games she and Chryssie had played. Later, they'd meet up with the gang at Clearwater Beach, drink sodas, eat chips and play volleyball until sunset. That was the life. Carefree. Spirited.

After graduation, while Angela attended college, Chryssie traveled the world on her trust fund—and had a baby. As the proud godmother, Angela tracked Danae Hart's growth through a series of snapshots and occasional visits. Then, only days after her first promotion at Waynscot, Angela got the call that told her Chryssie was dead. Thankfully, Dani, a precocious four-year-old, hadn't been in the car on the slippery Napa Valley road. Without hesitation, Angela became a single parent.

A shout and a ball hit in her direction brought Angela back to the game. She dove across the sand, digging the ball upward just in time for Lisa Holcomb to spike it over for a point.

"Great move, Ange!" shouted teammate Sammy Dugan, extending a hand to help her up.

"Thanks. I'd forgotten the sweet taste of sand between my teeth," she quipped, fighting the reflex to spit. She didn't think Jack would find that particularly arousing. As she slapped the sand off her thighs, Jack sent her an appreciative wink.

"Listen, why don't we take a break?" Sammy suggested. "I need to talk to you about something."

Without much prodding, two sideline observers jumped in to take their spots while Angela retrieved her towel and Sammy bought fruit juices at the cabana. She spotted Jack lowering his sunglasses and watching her narrowly—until the competition nearly crowned him with a well-aimed serve.

Sammy was divorced and available, but not Angela's type. He never had been, and they'd known each other since the fourth grade. Of course, that hadn't stopped Jack from accusing her of flirting with Sammy at the prom.

"So, Sam, what's up?" She slid onto a cabana bar stool.

"It's about tonight."

"The dinner? You and our former senior class officers have everything under control. Everything's been first rate so far."

"Thanks, and we do. It's just, well, we have a slide show planned for tonight, and I thought I should talk to you since we sort of have a tribute to Chryssie Hart worked in."

Angela took a deep swallow of her pineapple cocktail. From the beach, she heard someone yell, "Game point."

"I mean, maybe we should have talked to you first. You were her best friend."

"Yeah, Sammy, I think that would've been a good idea. I don't mean to cause a problem or anything, but you know, if Chryssie was still alive, I don't think she would have come this weekend. I wasn't just her best friend. I was her only friend."

Almost her only friend. Her gaze found Jack as he smashed the ball over the net for the win.

"A lot of people thought highly of her."

"Before or after she died?"

She didn't mean to be cruel, but protecting Chryssie's memory was second nature to her. Chryssie was Dani's birth mother, after all.

Sammy took a long sip from his glass. "The reunion committee just thought since she's the only one in our class to pass on, we should do something."

"How big of you all." She didn't disguise her acrimony. She couldn't. Chryssie would've said a lot worse. "And before that magnanimous decision was made, how many wisecracks were made about her reputation? How many off-color stories were told?"

Beneath his blooming sunburn, Sammy blushed. "People can be really stupid sometimes."

Angela took another sip and let the sweet, cool liquid slide down her throat. She'd been close to Sammy in high school, but despite his leadership position, he'd followed the crowd without much protest—probably accounting for his popularity. Deep down, he was a good soul, and he probably meant well, but the last thing she needed tonight was Chryssie's ghost.

She placed her hand atop Sammy's and turned on her brightest smile. "As Chryssie's best friend, I appreciate the thought. But she hated hypocrites more than anything else in the world. If it's not too much to ask, I'd like that segment of the slide show edited out before tonight, okay?"

Sammy nodded shyly. "For some reason, I thought you might feel that way. I should have asked you before today."

"That's okay. I appreciate the consideration. In her own twisted way, I think Chryssie would have, too."

He excused himself, but only after obtaining a promise from Angela to dance with him that evening. She remained at the bar, nursing her drink and considering adding rum to dispel the increasingly annoying déjà vu that seemed to be haunting the day.

Chryssie hated hypocrites. Then how could she have been one? Even the sugary fruit juice couldn't cover the bitterness that filled Angela all over again.

"It's a little early for piña coladas, isn't it?"

She held up her hands innocently. "It's virgin, cross my heart."

Jack leaned in and stole a swig. "You or the drink?"

"You know the answer to that."

Casually, he slid in beside her and ordered a club soda with a twist. Silence passed until the drink arrived.

"So, what did Sammy want?"

"Me. What else?"

Jack swiveled and leaned back with his elbows on the imitation tiki bar. "That makes two of us."

"After the way you left this morning, I wasn't so sure."

He tilted his drink toward her in a salute. "This morning wasn't about *not* wanting you, angel." He lowered his voice. "It was about wanting you so much I couldn't move."

She maneuvered her straw into her mouth and sucked in, savoring the cold. Funny how quickly a throat could get parched.

"Hey—" Jack's voice resumed its regular volume "—what's this I hear about Chryssie Hart?"

Angela reached into her beach bag and withdrew a tube of lip balm. "She's become a real topic of conver-

sation today. I guess people are finally taking note of
who's here and who's not." She smoothed the emollient
over her mouth with deliberate quickness.

"I heard she died."

"Six years ago."

"I didn't know. I'm sorry."

She couldn't help feeling chastised by the sincerity in
his voice. Although she had loads of evidence to prove
the indifference of her classmates toward Chryssie, she
didn't have a shred to hold against Jack. In fact, she had
just the opposite.

"Thanks. Chryssie didn't have any family left, and
she died in California. She left instructions in her will
for me to keep all the arrangements very private. The
only person I called was Richard Lassiter, and he must
have told the school. Her death was briefly mentioned
in the alumni newsletter a year later."

"Richard Lassiter." Jack spoke the words slowly, as if
conjuring a picture in his mind with each syllable. "He
was a couple of years ahead of us in school. Is he still
around?"

*My, oh, my, but isn't this conversation going down the
wrong road?*

"He runs an art gallery in Fort Lauderdale."

Jack started talking about a gallery in Lauderdale that
had once shown his photographs, and with only a little
prodding from her, the discussion moved away from
Chryssie and Richard. With relief, she noted he hadn't
asked about Dani, and to date, neither had anyone else.
She'd never gone out of her way to hide Dani's parentage—at least not the maternal side—but few people
knew Angela had a daughter, much less the love child
of the class bad girl. The few people who did know either didn't have the nerve to ask Angela any personal

questions or assumed that Angela—not Chryssie—had given birth so soon after graduation.

And that assumption was fine with her.

"Is everything okay?" Jack asked after a lull in their conversation. "You look a little...serious."

"Do I?"

She knew she did. The day hadn't started off simple and had only become more complicated. She took a quick peek at her watch. *Saved by the bell.*

"Well," she said, taking one last sip of her drink and gathering her bag, "I have a remedy."

Jack smirked and lifted his eyebrows suggestively. "So do I, but I promised the guys a rematch."

"Don't get cocky, buddy boy, or you'll be doing nothing but dreaming about me for another ten years."

He choked on his last sip. "Thanks for the warning. Where are you going?"

"I've got a date...with a masseuse and a steam bath. Too bad you're busy and can't come along." She moved in as close as she could, so her breath cooled the sweat on his neck. "You'll just have to play the game in the hot sun, while I'm lying naked on the table, only a towel and some very slick, very oily lotion and a man's big hands to keep me warm."

He licked his lips.

Mission accomplished.

"You, Angela Harris, are evil."

She couldn't suppress her girlish giggle or the lightened lilt in her walk as she sauntered away. Tonight should prove to be very interesting.

4

THE MASSEUSE, a large, matronly woman dressed entirely in white and smiling as if she'd just won the lottery, calmed Angela's nerves even before she climbed on the table. She'd never admit it to Jack, but Angela preferred all masculine touching to be done by him alone. Though they'd been together for less than twenty-four hours, his touch kindled feelings of both safety and desperate peril—keeping her guessing, anticipating. She hadn't been this out-of-control in years. The fear was there, but it felt good.

After her sauna, a shower and an extended lunch with former classmates, Angela retreated to her room and checked her voice mail. Dani's message lightened her mood, though she did switch on the weather channel to monitor the rain Dani reported had caused the cancellation of the white-water rafting trip.

Satisfied the showers were unfortunate but nonthreatening, Angela spent the next few hours putting the finishing touches on Monday's proposal, outlining her firm's surefire business plan to introduce her client's product—a ritzy housing development—to south Florida home buyers. When her eyes glazed over, she shut her laptop and pushed business from her mind. She dressed at a leisurely pace, poured herself a glass of wine from the minibar and sauntered onto the balcony.

The beach, nearly deserted as evening encroached,

lulled her with its music. Gulls cawed from the expanse of lavender sky, and the changing tide sloshed against the sand in perfect rhythm.

The sunset darkened the gulf to a deep plum color rimmed with ripples of fire, reminding her of Jack's touch—a touch she already missed. How could her plan possibly work? How would she remove the man from her memory if being with him only increased his presence there?

As if her thought was a summoner's spell, a knock reverberated against the door.

A tremor shimmied up her spine. She crossed the suite quickly, opened the door and stopped dead. Brazenly, she eyed him up and down. Her mouth lost moisture. Their mutually appreciative stares met in the middle.

She managed a breathless, "Wow."

Dressed in a tailored, vestless tuxedo and collarless shirt, he appeared as cosmopolitan as his professional life-style demanded. He'd slicked back the sides of his light brown hair, leaving the top slightly tousled as if blown by a nonexistent wind. The effect was pulse-fluttering.

"Right back at you," he responded.

She retreated, sweeping aside the short train of her gown and opening the door wider. As he crossed the threshold, he pulled a nosegay of deep purple violets and the tiniest pink tea roses from behind his back.

She accepted the flowers shyly, inhaling the sweet scent.

"I always loved violets." She ran her finger gently over one of the petals. "Roses, too."

Jack shoved his hands into his pockets. "I remembered."

"How thoughtful of you." She closed the door behind him. "I mean, you didn't have to go to this trouble. Thank you."

"Angela, you and I—together—that's trouble we can't avoid. We might as well just give in and enjoy the ride."

He doesn't know the half of it, she thought, walking to the darkened bedroom to retrieve her purse.

"The violets match my gown. Did you peek in my closet?"

His voice followed her. "You always favored purple for formal occasions. In the spirit of things, I took a chance."

A familiar wave of apprehension overtook her. She checked her makeup in the mirror by the light from the other room. She reached into her handbag and extracted a tube of lipstick to apply another layer to her wine-tinted lips.

"Don't add another stroke," he said, his voice heavy with quiet authority.

Looking past her reflection, she saw him standing directly behind her.

"You look perfect. You don't need anything, except maybe a long, wet, drawn-out kiss to add a little natural color."

She twisted the tube closed. "Is that what I need?"

He licked his lips. "That and much more. Much more."

Taking her elbow, he turned her around. He ran his hand up her arm, over her full-length satin gloves to the short sleeves hanging loose below her shoulders. When he reached her neck, he slipped his fingers into her hair.

"I like your hair down."

Pressing her lips together, she wondered if they'd

make the dinner. She also considered whether or not she cared. The color of his eyes darkened to a rich emerald, and he stepped closer to her, slipping his other hand to the small of her back.

The warmth of his palm heated the clingy silk of her gown. As the fever spread through her, coiling in the center of her feminine core, she leaned toward him.

"What else do you like?" she asked, nuzzling her cheek to his, inhaling the crisp citrus scent of his aftershave.

He whistled long and low, sending his warm breath skittering over her skin. "I like knowing how much you want me."

She leaned back, her eyebrows raised in semishock. True or not, the admission sounded entirely too confident. "Didn't I warn you about getting too cocky?"

Tightening his hold, he pressed his lips against her temple. "Yes, but that's what you do to me. If you'd shown me ten years ago that you wanted me, we might never have been apart."

She laughed skeptically, then kissed him playfully on the chin. Cocky or not, he did have her nerve endings crackling with more electricity than a power plant. The sensation, invigorating and addictive, spurred instant forgiveness for his bravado.

"You know that's not true," she said. "If I'd showed you then how much I wanted you, we would have slept together a few times in the back seat of your Mustang, and the magic would have died an uneventful death. I would have become just another one of your conquests."

His shoulders tensed and his spine stiffened before he pushed her gently away. Without his body heat, she shivered.

"Let's go." He stepped toward the door, his voice soft, accompanied by a teasing smile. "We don't want to be late, do we?"

She grabbed her purse and followed. "I don't care if we go or not." Standing inches from him, she felt a chasm building that left her chilled and confused. She hadn't said anything insulting. She had spoken the hard truth—one he obviously didn't want to face. And she thought she'd been the only one to romanticize the past.

He took her hand and placed a weightless kiss on her palm.

"I want to escort you the way I should have done prom night. With a little patience. And a lot more style. I'm a changed man, angel. At least, I could be, with you at my side." He entwined her arm in his and led her out of the suite.

She smiled, not knowing what else to do or say. Jack's changing—truly changing—hadn't been a factor in her weekend fling. Yet the more time she spent with him, the more she witnessed the scope of his transformation.

He wasn't a hormone-driven kid anymore, interested only in sex and turning his back on love.

He was a man. Complicated. Charming. Terrifying.

Sexy as hell.

They didn't speak when they entered the elevator, and luckily, former classmates joined them and filled the strained silence with chatter. Angela turned aside when she caught the naughty glimmer in Jack's eyes and silently chastised herself for entertaining the erotic thoughts his lusty expression inspired. Until that moment, *Fatal Attraction* had been one of her least favorite movies.

As they exited, Jack leaned in and whispered,

"Maybe we ought to take the stairs on the way back. Elevators do weird things to people."

She shook her head. "I'm not opposed to weird, are you?"

His chuckle disappeared beneath the music blaring from the bandstand. A hostess escorted them to their table, seating them with Mike Nichols, his wife, Jeanette, Sammy Dugan and his date. Angela ordered a glass of Zinfandel and tried to ignore the raised eyebrows and sidelong glances around the table when Jack nonchalantly laid his hand over hers.

"So," Jeanette said, after a generous gulp of her vodka martini, "Mike tells me you two were an item back in school. Things heating up again?"

Angela answered by grinning, swallowing a mouthful of wine and fighting the urge to pull her hand from Jack's grasp. But she didn't. Not because she didn't want to look like a trapped fox but because she liked the warm pressure of his touch.

Jack fielded the question with practiced finesse. "How can I resist a woman like Angela? She'll probably just break my heart again." He punctuated his compliment by raising her hand to his lips and brushing a kiss across her knuckles.

Obviously impressed, Jeanette turned her attention to her husband, chastised him for not being romantic, then told them how her hapless husband had proposed. Angela laughed in all the appropriate places, as did Jack, but her mind barely registered the details of the story. She doubted his did, either.

Smoldering, his gaze met and held hers. His stare stroked her with longing, perused her with desire and set her heart to fluttering so that only looking away and swallowing more wine kept her from dragging him straight to that elevator.

Just before the main course, Sammy excused himself to play emcee. He took a microphone from the bandleader, thanked the reunion committee for their efforts and invited former teachers to stand and receive applause.

Angela tried to be politely attentive, but Jack had scooted nearer to her and draped his arm possessively across the back of her chair. His body heat warmed her, and the scent of his cologne made her crave a juicy bite of orange.

"And now I'd like to open nominations from the floor for the winner of our most unusual job award," Sammy announced, snapping Angela's attention to him as a spotlight flared from the corner.

"Should I nominate you?" Jack asked.

"Me? I'm in marketing. So are a dozen other people." She eyed him warily, suspicious of his motives—particularly when she caught the roguish glimmer dancing in his green eyes.

"I wasn't talking about that job. I thought I might nominate you for the job you're doing on me this weekend. How should I phrase it? Professional temptress? What about ache-maker?"

"Jack," she chastised, feeling herself redden in a blush only he could see. "I'll nominate you for a few awards, too, if you're not careful."

"Like what? Most likely to make a fool of himself in front of his ex-girlfriend?"

The audience, laughing and applauding, voted by clapping for the winner, an on-air personality for a home shopping network.

"You've never been a fool in my eyes, Jack. Now or then."

Jack grabbed his iced tea and took a deep swallow. "That just shows how little you know about me."

Angela slid her wineglass nearer, letting his comment die under Sammy's voice.

"Next up, let's hear nominations for the person who traveled the farthest to see us all again."

Angela considered Jack for this category, since he'd come from an assignment in Dublin, but she thought better of it when sharp bitterness darkened Jack's expression. She wondered about his comment but never for a moment considered asking him to explain. Casual lovers didn't talk of such things. They flirted. They bantered. They spoke in hushed tones about pleasures of the body, not secrets of the soul.

"Maybe they'll vote for the most changed person," she said once the crease in his forehead softened.

"Would you win, or would I?"

She sipped her wine as the crowd chose a former classmate who lived in Zaire. "I haven't changed so much."

Jack chuckled and shook his head. "You're kidding, right?" Amused disbelief erased the last of his seriousness, and his delight irked her. She frowned.

"I meant that as a compliment, angel. Every change you've made has been for the better. You shouldn't have one regret."

That just shows how little you know about me, her mind echoed. She snapped the napkin on her lap free of nonexistent crumbs. "I could say the same to you."

His grin lit his eyes. "Then let's call it a toss-up." He kissed her sweetly on the cheek as the lights went up and the server arrived with their meal.

After dinner, the band played tunes, some fast, some slow, from their senior year. With only the first few notes, Angela recognized their song, a sultry ballad about lost and found love. She tried to involve herself in a conversation, pick at the last remnants of her dessert—anything to keep Jack from asking her to dance. Her memories had become raw wounds. Dancing would salt them with a decade's unshed tears.

Yet she couldn't resist. When he stood, moved her chair and touched her shoulder, she choked back a sob and took his hand.

Surrounded by a burgeoning mass of dancers, Angela slid her arms around his neck and rested her head against his chest. For an instant, she wondered if Jack meant to dance at all, since he held her still and unmoving. Then he took her right hand in his left, pressing it against his chest as they swayed.

Immediately, Jack regretted asking her to dance. The scent of her skin mingling with her perfume mocked him. Her warmth teased him. Her shivering grabbed him at the center of his heart. This woman held entirely too much power over his responses, his thoughts, his memories. And yet, he couldn't resist her any more than he could a muted sunset or an ethereal shaft of sunlight making halos out of branches and leaves. Those images he captured with his camera. Angela he'd capture with his touch.

The idea had struck him earlier, as he'd decided that resisting Angela was futile. He could turn her plan against her. She'd come to the reunion for a weekend of indulgence, to enjoy what she'd missed on prom night, thanks to his petty jealousy. He hadn't missed the irony that they'd been seated with Sammy Dugan—the boy he'd been jealous of all those years ago.

But tonight would be different. Very different.

Angela shifted, turning her hand in his, reminding him that dancing required movement. He complied, listening to the tempo and moving accordingly. But the gentle pressure of her hand in his, the smooth, scented skin of her bare neck and shoulders, the sexy way her hips rocked beneath his hand destroyed his timing. He stopped, captured her gaze with his, then smiled.

The blatant desire in her hazel eyes matched his. Without a word, he led her off the crowded dance floor and out of the ballroom. If not for the elderly couple occupying the elevator when they got on, they might not have made it to her room.

The minute the door of her suite closed behind them, she was in his arms, pressed to him so that nothing separated them but their clothes. Jack sought to rectify that immediately. He shrugged out of his jacket, unbuttoned the top button of his shirt and lowered the zipper on the back of her dress.

Stepping back, he held her still. As if his gaze was a camera, he snapped a shot. Her hair cascaded in wanton curls, caressing the curves of her bare shoulders. Her lips were slightly swollen from their recent kiss, and her eyes glittered with unharnessed desire. His heart lurched at the idea that this could be their last night together—if she had her way.

Which she wouldn't.

"You are so beautiful. No one held a candle to you tonight. No one."

She lowered her arms, allowing her bodice to slip down and reveal a black, strapless merry widow.

He groaned appreciatively. Her attention to sensual detail fired him. His groin tightened.

Wordlessly, she bit the thumb of her right glove and tugged the material loose until it slid off her arm.

"Tonight is all we have left. Let's not waste a minute."

Jack pushed the dress over her hips until it pooled at her feet. Now wasn't the time to point out her misconception. He'd let her believe this was their last night together if that made her happy. Only he needed to know he'd developed a craving for her that couldn't be satisfied in a weekend. Only he needed to know he planned to make love to her so thoroughly that she wouldn't have the power to leave. She removed the other glove, dropping it on the floor just inside her bedroom door. He followed, stopping on the threshold to watch her climb onto the bed with the grace of a lioness. He tore away his shirt and pants, then rested beside her.

He grabbed her wrists and trapped them above her head. Kissing a path from her mouth to the breasts straining above the lacy trim of her lingerie, he inhaled her spiced scent and felt his mind whirl.

He licked her nipple when her labored breathing brought her breast to his mouth. Shifting his weight and leaving one hand securely around her wrists, he tugged the merry widow down and laved her until the velvety nub puckered tight.

Angela closed her eyes, releasing her mind and body to his control. His breath and lips and tongue fanned her need for him like dry air to a lit match. He cupped her breasts, kissing them, kneading them, making her experience every sensation to the fullest—from whisper soft to biting rough.

He released her wrists, needing both hands to lift her forward and undo the tiny hooks tracing her spine. She thrust her hands into his hair, pulling his mouth to hers, savoring the taste of his power and the scent of his desire.

Flinging her lingerie aside, he sat back, moving his hands down her rib cage until he clasped the edge of her panties. Easing down on the bed, he inched the material away. She closed her eyes again, unable to watch his hungry eyes as they feasted on her so boldly.

His weight lifted from the bed just as he snapped the panties from her ankle.

"Open your eyes, Angela."

His command was impossible to ignore. Her gaze locked with his, and she employed all her will to restrain the urge to grab the bedspread and cover herself. Never had anyone looked at her with such uncontrolled longing.

"You're so perfect."

His assessment sapped her breath. "You're so far away."

When he grabbed the edge of his briefs, she glanced aside.

"Angela." Her name was a reprimand.

She returned her attention to him, biting her bottom lip as he slid the cotton down, revealing himself fully.

"I'm so ready for you."

His announcement was unnecessary but succeeded in heightening the anticipation flowing through her. When he bent forward to kiss her toes, a tiny gasp escaped her lips. As he traced a moist path around her ankle, over her calf, beneath her kneecap, inside her lower thigh, she thought she'd scream.

"Are you as ready for me?"

He spoke the question with his mouth hovering at the base of her thighs. His breath made her quiver. His hands eased her legs apart.

"Jack, I..." She lost her voice when he dipped a finger inside her.

"You're so sweet and slick. How does this feel?"

She couldn't answer. Her senses focused on the intimate stroke of his fingers and the accompanying flicks of his tongue. Grasping his hair, she tried to pull him away, tried without conviction to deny herself the delicious ecstasy shooting through her every vein.

"Jack, please," she pleaded.

"Please what? Please stop?"

He pressed deeper. She cried out. Colors bold and bright sizzled behind her eyes, and she nearly bucked off the bed. He held her hips still and tongued her thoroughly.

She managed to mutter only two words.

"Don't stop."

He chuckled and raised himself over her. "I don't intend to stop, Angela. Not until dawn. Maybe not even then."

"GOOD MORNING."

Angela jumped, startled by Jack's sleepy voice. She closed her suitcase and turned to find him leaning seductively across the bed. Okay, maybe he was just lying there, but he had a knack for making the simplest expression look very seductive.

"Good morning to you. You sure do sleep soundly. I showered, dressed and packed, and you didn't so much as snore."

"What can I say?" His eyes twinkled devilishly. "You wore me out, lady."

She turned away, despite the fact that the room's dimness covered her blush.

"Come here."

She zipped her suitcase, set it on the chair and grasped the handle like an anchor. She'd secretly hoped to gather her things and leave before he awoke, avoiding the morning-after scene she now faced. Though he'd fallen into a sleep resembling a coma around four o'clock, she'd spent the better part of what was left of the darkness staring out the sliding glass doors, reliving every delectable detail of their lovemaking—every kiss, every touch, every condom. Her body ached in places she never knew could ache.

"I don't think that's a good idea." She clutched the handle tighter. As morning dawned, she'd made a decision about Jack. She had to stick to her choice.

She heard the rustle as he threw the sheets aside, the jingle of his pants as he eased them on, the soft padding of his feet against the carpet as he walked up behind her. She had ample time to escape, but that meant turning around and staring into those consuming eyes.

"Didn't work, did it?"

Drawing in a deep breath, she swung around indignantly. "What are you talking about?"

He ran his hand along her cheek and fought to contain his impertinent grin. "Your plan to have a weekend fling."

Grabbing her suitcase, she swung it around, causing him to jump back or be pummeled by its weight.

"I hate to break the news, Sullivan, but my scheme worked like a charm."

She balanced the luggage against her hip and made her way to the other room. He didn't follow, but leaned against the doorjamb while she dialed the front desk for a bellman. She counted the rings, trying to ignore the weight of his stare on her bare back. She cursed herself for not packing a few of her usual oversize T-shirts along with her intentionally skimpy wardrobe.

After placing her request with the front desk, she dialed room service and ordered him breakfast. In his room.

"There." She grabbed her purse from the table and slung the strap over her shoulder. "You'd better dress and return to your room or you'll miss your morning meal."

Jack shot forward and gathered her in his arms before she had time to react. His bare arms, still warm and scented with the fragrance of their lovemaking, ensnared her like a steel trap. "I'd much rather have you for breakfast."

"I bet you would." Her sarcasm faltered under the strength of his embrace and the intensity of his hungry gaze. She could easily surrender and let him lead her to the bed—to give in to the throbbing ache he'd renewed in her with a simple touch. But she wouldn't. The battle was won. The war was over.

She braced her hands on his chest and tried to push away. "Jack, please."

He lifted his eyebrow, causing her to remember how she'd used those same words just the night before.

"We both got what we wanted last night," she insisted, forcing herself to meet his gaze straight on. "Our reunion is over and done with."

She hoped the dismissal would free her without further discussion. The determined set of his jaw and the gleam in his eyes told her she didn't stand a chance.

"Over and done with?" He chuckled and placed a placating kiss on the top of her forehead. "Not in my book, angel."

"Take a hint, Jack." She yanked her arms out of his hold and disengaged herself from his warmth.

Until he'd awoken, she'd done nothing but think about their lovemaking. Without doubt, Jack roused passions she never knew existed. She needed to save those desires for someone who wasn't a threat to her daughter or the life she'd so carefully shaped. "This may be a first for you, but my desire for you is sated. I don't suppose you've ever experienced someone using you and setting you aside after a few nights of pleasure...."

"No, I haven't." He shoved his hands in his pockets. An inkling of vulnerability laced his words like a sprinkling of arsenic—nearly undetectable yet dangerous to ingest. "Neither have you."

She shifted her weight, uncomfortable with how waspish she sounded. "Fair enough." She lowered her voice, attempting to drain all the spite from it. "That doesn't change the fact that you want something from me I can't give. You want the woman I used to be. She's gone. She grew up."

He traced his finger over her blouse, outlining her cleavage. She willed herself not to move, not to react. His intoxicating effect over her was finished, right?

"She's grown up, all right. Enough to know what she really needs."

"Yes." Her voice grew raspy as his thumb passed over her nipple. She stepped back and crossed her arms over her chest. "And I don't need you. I can't."

"Then what was last night? And the night before?" He stepped forward slowly, his intense gaze gluing her to the spot. "You think our passion came from an old memory. Maybe we started that way—" he dislodged her hands from her protective stance and rubbed the tension out of her knuckles "—but we're not done yet."

After placing tender kisses on both palms, he snapped a business card out of his wallet and slipped it into her purse. "When you admit the truth to yourself, whether today or next week or next year, you know where to find me."

He disappeared into the darkness of the bedroom as the bellman knocked on the door. He stood, just out of sight while she hesitated. He heard her take the card out of the purse. A minute later she answered the door, instructed the bellman to take her bag and left.

He hadn't expected her to walk away. Maybe he was losing his touch. Maybe Angela didn't need him as much as he needed her. Maybe he hadn't pleased her...hadn't touched the depths of her soul with his lovemaking.

Nah.

Jack swept his shirt from the floor and shrugged into it before housekeeping showed up to prep the room for the next guest. He sat on the bed to slide on his shoes, then let himself lie back in the tangled sheets, inhaling the scent of Angela's natural perfume, recalling the fearless way she responded to his every intimate touch. What they'd shared had been special. Unique. Unforgettable. He just had to wait for her to realize it, too.

Though her adventurous air surprised him, he'd caught hints of the shyness she tried so hard to hide— the way she glanced sidelong when he first suckled her breasts, the way her hands quivered when he caressed her, the way she tugged her bottom lip with her teeth when he employed some new, erotic touches. The longer they'd been together, the more her intrinsic naiveté shone through, making his heart soar. He swelled with renewed desire.

He finished dressing quickly, knowing he'd go stark, raving mad if he stayed in her room. As battle-scarred as he was with women and sex, he was humbled by how his responses to Angela were so fresh and raw. The results were downright rejuvenating—just what he'd come home for.

If she really thought their time together was over, she had another think coming. As far as he was concerned, the reunion had just begun.

5

"HE DID WHAT?"

Angela didn't need her assistant, Nancy Brennan, to repeat herself. She'd heard what Nancy had said. She just didn't want to believe it.

What a great way to start a Monday. Angela glanced around her home office and checked the clock. Eight o'clock. She'd returned early on Sunday, but she'd spent most of the day unpacking, doing laundry and trying not to think about Jack. The last thing she wanted to worry about was work. She'd checked her messages religiously, and everything seemed to be business as usual. Until this phone call.

"I'm really sorry, Angela. None of us saw this coming," Nancy said, her young, barely-out-of-college voice brimming with sincerity—and a touch of fear. This could mean job losses. Layoffs. Bankruptcy.

"Well, I certainly didn't, and watching out for the company is *my* responsibility, not yours." Angela chastised herself for getting so wrapped up in Jack and the reunion that one of her associates had the time and the temerity to resign and take her biggest client and two assistants with him. "Are any of his other files missing?"

The shuffling of papers echoed over the phone line.

"The Whispering Palms file isn't here," Nancy answered, her voice weak with worry.

"Wonderful." Angela tried to keep the tapping of her fingers from resembling the machine-gun fire she'd like to level at the traitor, Randall Hautman. "Call Mr. Davenport at Whispering Palms immediately and confirm our eleven o'clock appointment. Assure him I have a really stellar presentation for him."

"Randall wouldn't dare go after that account." Nancy attempted to reassure both Angela and herself. "If he takes Whispering Palms, we're—"

"Through." Angela finished the thought. "Randall's not stupid. We only have a tentative contract with Whispering Palms. They paid for and received the marketing analysis. We can't take for granted we'll win the promotion and advertising job. Randall could, theoretically, slip in right now and steal Davenport away. We can't afford to lose this one. I've upgraded equipment. Hired more staff."

Angela switched on her home computer and dialed the office modem.

"Confirm the appointment, Nan," Angela continued once she'd tapped in her password, "and double-check every file in Randall's desk. And mine. Make sure nothing else is missing. In fact, why don't you set up meetings for me with all our major clients. Don't start them until Wednesday. Breakfasts, lunches, dinners, I don't care. But I need time for damage control on Whispering Palms before I take care of everyone else."

"What about Styler Jewels? Do you want to try to get them back?"

Angela stretched her neck as the computer file for Styler Jewels, the purloined company, popped onto her screen. "It's probably a lost cause by now, but I'll make that call myself. You just get in touch with Davenport.

And remember, tell him I have something huge planned for him."

"Sure, Angela, I'll get right on it. But..."

Angela had already started reviewing the Styler account when Nancy's nervous silence gained her attention. "But what, Nan?"

"What do you have planned?"

Inhaling deeply, Angela questioned the caliber of Harris and Associates' latest bid for the promotion of Whispering Palms. The pitch, slick enough to reach the target audience yet classy enough to flow with Davenport's reputation, contained major strengths, easily outdoing anything she'd seen before. But what about the weaknesses? What if she'd been so wrapped up in her anticipation of seeing Jack that she'd ignored a vital angle or missed a unique slant?

She pushed her uncertainty away. Angela knew marketing. She'd spent her entire professional career studying companies, recommending promotional and growth tactics, then implementing those strategies with her team of creative professionals. She'd been successful. She could do this.

"I'm presenting the proposal we put together last week. I only hope it's good enough to wow the man's socks off."

WHEN ALLISTAIR DAVENPORT left Angela's south Tampa office, his socks were still firmly affixed to his feet. Though he hadn't nixed Angela's campaign entirely, he demanded more—something spectacular, he'd said—from the firm who wanted to take over his multimillion-dollar account.

Angela spent the rest of the afternoon brainstorming with her creative team, throwing out and batting away ideas until just before her four o'clock meeting with David Styler. In a rare move, she dismissed the staff early. Tired and shocked by Randall's betrayal, they were too distracted to produce the kind of campaign Davenport wanted.

After a brief and unsuccessful meeting with Styler, she drove to see her accountant—a move she regretted as she maneuvered her Pathfinder down busy Tampa streets toward home. Losing Styler Jewels had hurt the bottom line more than she cared to admit, thanks to investments she'd made to secure the Davenport Homes account. For the first time since she'd started her business, financial vulnerability threatened her future.

How could she have been so blind? How could she not have guessed Randall's duplicity? How could she have presented a less than perfect proposal when her business depended on success?

As she pulled into the garage and turned off the ignition, one name answered all her questions.

Jack.

Clearly, it wasn't fair to blame him for her misfortune. However, even today, while fighting for her company's survival, she'd found herself remembering the way he crooked his knuckle beneath her chin when he kissed her, reliving the tense anticipation of his lips trailing down her neck, hearing the echo of his voice gasping her name with erotic release.

Jack wasn't any further out of her system than the blood pumping through her veins.

As she reached into her closet after her shower, a frightening inspiration hit her. Hung in the dry, dark space for preservation, the little violet and rose bouquet sparked an image that could change her future—privately and professionally. Allistair Davenport, a developer and entrepreneur, was respected for his knowledge of popular art. No doubt the man knew photography as well as sculpture and painting.

Even before Jack's face made the tabloids, thanks to his association with supermodel Lily Dee, he'd been widely recognized for his talent. His unique photographs of the Florida Everglades were used by conservationalists worldwide. The U.S. Postal Service used his sunset shot of the Painted Desert in a limited-edition stamp. A showing in New York two summers ago elicited critical acclaim, clearly distinguishing him from countless camera jocks and putting his work on the cover of *New York* magazine.

Jack Sullivan was truly spectacular—in more ways than one.

She couldn't. Her idea was too risky. Ill-advised. Dangerous.

Still... It could save her business.

A minute later, she'd found Jack's business card.

"Sullivan here," he answered, breathing hard, as if he'd raced to the phone.

She thanked heaven some idiot inventor hadn't yet come up with a cost-effective videophone. "How sweet. You're out of breath and you didn't even know it was me," she teased, while shaking like a leaf from head to toe.

His laugh from the other end was deep-throated and low. "I must have a sixth sense for sexy women."

And a lucky streak a mile long, Jack added silently. Balancing the phone with his shoulder, he wiped his suddenly sweaty hands on his jeans. He'd been thinking about Angela all morning as he unpacked his equipment and settled into his new home. He wondered about how she'd spent her day yesterday, and mostly how she'd spent the night.

Did she really consider their reunion a weekend fling? Or had he branded himself deeper into her soul, as she had with him? He decided he might never know unless he came up with an excuse to see or call her.

Now she had called him. Why?

"What's up?" he asked, plopping into a worn chair he'd inherited with his new warehouse-office-home.

"Oh, Jack, you walk right into them, don't you? Nothing is up—yet, but I'm working on it." She punctuated her innuendo with a giggle.

He shifted in his seat, amazed how the sound of her voice could make him hard. She'd waltzed into dangerous territory—Jack's home turf. "Do you need a few ideas, or do you have some of your own?"

"I don't give away my secrets that easily. Anticipation is a powerful ally."

"I won't have to wait another ten years, will I?"

She laughed. "How about an hour? I'll bring dinner if you haven't already eaten. You can show me your studio."

"I haven't eaten, and I'm starved." *For you.* "But are you sure you want to venture into my lair?"

"I'm an adventurer at heart, Jack. Didn't you know that?"

After a few moments, the conversation ended, but Jack remained in his chair with the phone on his chest. He'd hoped she'd call him, but he never anticipated he'd hear from her so soon. She had invited herself over for a reason—a good reason. He knew her well enough to know she wouldn't change her mind about seeing him again without strong motivation.

He also knew to answer the door when opportunity

knocked. She wanted something from him, something she'd swallow her pride to get. He wanted something, as well, and luckily, bargaining and bartering were pastimes he enjoyed.

She claimed to be an adventurer at heart. Good. Jack hoped her words would prove true. For tonight, she'd need every ounce of daring she had to meet him.

With a bass chuckle, he pushed out of the chair and got to work.

ANGELA SET THE PHONE on its cradle just in time to hear her sister singing her familiar, "Knock, knock," greeting.

"Door's open, Kell," Angela shouted from her bedroom, scurrying to shut the closet before her sister spotted the wilting corsage. She didn't have time to fill Kelly in on the reunion, not that she had any intention of telling her about Jack. However, she didn't want to lie. Her best bet was to avoid the topic altogether.

Angela dug a fresh pair of panty hose out of her lingerie drawer as Kelly stuck her head around the door frame. "Hey, sis." Her expression, dominated by round, brown eyes, twisted with disappointment when she noticed the fresh suit laid out on the bed. "I thought you were taking the night off. I wanted to invite you to dinner so you could fill me in on all the reunion gossip."

Kicking off her slippers, Angela sat on the bed and stuffed her feet into the hose, pulling them up quickly and trying not to remember how Jack had slithered similar lingerie off her only three nights before.

"I was, but I've got less than an hour to get to an appointment and try to arrange some damage control."

"Sounds serious." Kelly took Angela's blouse off the

hanger and helped her maneuver the silk over her head without smearing her makeup.

"Very." Angela tucked the blouse into her skirt and then shrugged on the jacket.

While Kelly wandered aimlessly around the room, picking up perfume bottles she'd sniffed countless times before, Angela brushed out her hair, twisting and securing it with a conservative tortoiseshell clip.

"I could've killed Garrett for forcing me to go to that home show yesterday." Kelly dabbed on some Chanel. "I'm dying to hear who married who, who lost hair, who was the best-looking single guy left."

When Kelly's roaming gaze neared the bedside table where she kept her phone, Angela's heart froze. Jack's business card lay beside it.

"Kelly!"

"What?"

Angela swallowed deeply, then spun around in her best quick recovery. "How does my hair look?"

Kelly stepped closer, away from the phone, to examine the back of Angela's head, smoothing a few loose ends. "Looks fine." She plopped down on the bed. "I've gotta tell you, Ange, I don't know if I like the boys being gone for two whole weeks. I'm bored out of my mind."

"You need a hobby." Angela palmed Jack's card and moved to the other side of the room. At one time, Kelly had thought Jack Sullivan was an all-right guy. But her opinion hadn't lasted long. As an older sister whose mother traveled three-quarters of the year, Kelly became responsible for little sister Angela's well-being. At the first hint that Jack wasn't a choirboy, Kelly decided Angela would be better off without him. And she hadn't been wrong—then or now. Angela didn't dare spill the beans about her weekend liaison to her maternally inclined sibling. Not until she was prepared for a lethal tongue-lashing.

Kelly propped a throw pillow under her head. "I've got it!"

Angela fastened the button on her jacket and smoothed a sheer shade of color over her lips.

"Got what?"

"A hobby." She laid back and tucked her hands comfortably behind her head. "I'll take the next two lonely weeks to concentrate on finding you a date."

Groaning, Angela replaced the cap on her lipstick and flung it into her tiny leather purse. "Why don't you try ceramics? The last thing I need after this weekend is a date."

She winced. That little admission would cost her plenty.

Kelly sat up on her elbows. "Oh, really?" She had a way of twisting those three syllables into an entire stanza of romantic assumption. "You know you aren't getting out of this house, appointment or not, without explaining that slip, sister dear."

Angela retreated to her closet to dig out matching leather pumps. Though she couldn't give her sister specifics—she'd die first—she felt the urgent need to talk, especially after she'd invited herself to Jack's for dinner. What she planned to do was reckless, impulsive, almost obsessive. Yet in the twenty-four hours since she'd left Jack in her hotel room, she couldn't get her mind off him. Even Randall Hautman's traitorous theft hadn't distracted her for more than thirty minutes. Instead, the situation gave her cause to see Jack again. And soon.

"So I met somebody this weekend," she admitted vacuously. She grabbed her briefcase from beside the door and headed down the hallway. "No big deal."

Kelly raced behind her. "Who?"

"You wouldn't remember him." She snagged a soda from the refrigerator and set it on the counter while she hunted for her insulated cup.

"Get your yearbook," Kelly insisted, popping open the can and taking a swig.

Angela snatched the drink away from her sister and poured the contents into the thermal container. "It's in the attic, and I need to leave here in—" she checked her watch "—five minutes."

Kelly pulled up a bar stool. "Then dish quickly."

"There's nothing to dish." She concentrated on the leak-proof cap, careful to cover the understatement. "We had a great time, and now it's over."

"Can you be any more vague than that? I mean, you shouldn't just give out the deep, dark intimate secrets of your life like that, sis."

"Ha, ha. It's just... Well, try as I may, I can't get the guy out of my head."

Kelly rolled her eyes, then brushed an errant brunette curl out of her face. "It's little wonder. You haven't had a real relationship for I don't know how long."

"I go out," Angela insisted, checking her answering machine and grabbing her car keys from the wooden key rack Dani had made at camp the previous year.

"On business. Since you adopted Dani, you only ask me to baby-sit for occasional one-time-only dates and a couple of client kiss-up dinners. Oh, wait." Kelly enhanced her exaggerated words with her hands palms up as if attempting to stop a speeding car. "There was that time two years ago when you dated the same guy twice. Of course, that ended after he hired your firm to promote his restaurant. I stand corrected."

"Cut the sarcasm." Angela escaped to the foyer. Sarcasm or not, Kelly was right. Since Chryssie's death, and maybe even before, Angela hadn't put much energy into her social life. So many other things came first—college, career, then Dani. When she did date, she tended to judge the men as potential fathers rather than as potential lovers. She hadn't regretted her choices until this weekend. Maybe if she'd been more experienced, Jack's effect on her wouldn't be so powerful.

"I admit I don't get around much." She checked the contents of her briefcase then snapped it shut. "I don't have time for meaningless dates. I've got a daughter to raise and a business to run."

"A daughter who might benefit from a father." Kelly joined her in the foyer, leaning on the doorjamb between the kitchen and the front hall with the same unwavering expression she wore whenever they broached this topic.

Angela glanced at her watch again. She had two minutes to navigate herself out of dangerous territory. "Dani doesn't need a father. She has Garrett for her male role model."

"It's not the same, Ange. Uncles are great, but she needs a father, preferably her own and preferably one who loves her mother."

Land mine number one.

"Speaking of fathers," Kelly continued. "Did Richard Lassiter show up at the reunion?"

"He graduated ahead of us. He had no reason to go."

Kelly nodded and Angela swallowed hard, feeling suddenly hot and stuffy in her breezy summer suit. Over a year ago, she'd tracked down Chryssie's exboyfriend, confident he was Dani's biological father. Chryssie never claimed he was, refusing to discuss the matter. But who else could Angela suspect? Then she'd found out about Richard's sterility, information she had shared with no one.

Kelly handed Angela her drink. "Have you decided whether or not to contact him about Dani?"

"I told you, Kelly, I'm going to abide by Chryssie's wishes. She didn't want Dani's father identified, so until I have a good reason, I'm letting the subject drop. Now look—" she changed the subject from one perilous topic to another "—do you want to know about my weekend or not?"

"How much time do I have left?"

"Sixty seconds and counting." She slung on the shoulder strap of her briefcase and poised her hand on the doorknob.

"Okay then tell me one thing about this guy you can't get out of your mind. Did you have a good time with him?"

A tingling sensation filtered through her. She'd had the most unbelievably delicious weekend of her life. "Like never before."

"Then see him again."

"Even if he may not be good for me? Or Dani?"

Kelly walked forward and placed a comforting hand on her sister's shoulder. "Leave Dani out of this for now. If you had a good time with him and he's male, he's good for you. Play the rest by ear."

Smiling indecisively, Angela opened the door and waved a wordless goodbye. The thick summer air coated her with wet warmth, making her squirm in her silk and linen. *Play the rest by ear.* The old Angela would never do that. She was too prepared, too analyzing, too cautious. Even in business, what may have looked to others as a bold and risky move would actually be a precisely calculated and executed plan.

The new Angela, the woman she'd become in Jack's presence, the sensual creature who craved Jack's touch, thrived on chance and uncertainty. The old Angela may have erased Jack from her system, but the new one had not. Unfortunately, the new one had to put her needs aside. Some risks were too dangerous to take.

BEFORE EXITING the car, Angela flipped open the vanity mirror on the sun visor. Staring straight into the depths of her hazel eyes, she pumped up her resolve. *This is it, Angela. As much as you hate to admit it, you need this man. You need him now. Go get him.*

Too bad what she needed him for was business.

Her meeting with David Styler of Styler Jewels had been a bust. Randall Hautman, her former associate, had done a world-class number on the guy. He'd convinced Styler beyond a doubt that Harris and Associates didn't understand his company's objectives and could no longer fulfill his marketing needs. Of course, Randy had also misinterpreted crucial numbers and inflated the value of his worth to the future of Styler Jewels.

Angela decided to look on the bright side. The account had never been her favorite. David Styler was a flake. She had to constantly cajole, entice and insist he make the right decisions for his company's well-being. Most of the time he listened. Sometimes he didn't. And now he'd proved his shortsightedness.

But she couldn't afford to lose Whispering Palms or its parent company, Davenport Homes. Allistair Davenport was no flake. The man was experienced. Savvy. Wealthy. His newest resort and housing community promised to make him wealthier, and Angela needed a piece of the action. She'd worked for over a

year to win Davenport's attention and six months more
for a tentative agreement on a contract. She wouldn't let
Randall abscond with this client and destroy her business without a war. An informant from Randy's new
firm verified a meeting between Davenport and Hautman for the end of the week. If Angela launched an attack, she would have to plan and execute her idea by
Wednesday at the latest.

And what better ammunition could she unload than
Jack Sullivan, the hottest photographer to emerge in
years?

She flipped the mirror closed and checked the empty
parking lot before she got out of her Pathfinder and set
the security alarm. Though Jack's lot was well lit, Ybor
City on a Monday night echoed with deserted silence.
The one-time heart of Tampa's Latin community had
experienced a marked rebirth, but on weekdays, the ac-
tivity in the business district died after the sun went
down.

The building, a renovated, three-story warehouse,
had few windows in the bottom floors, with the exception of a storefront still under construction. Conversely,
the top story had a consistent row of rectangular eyes
all awash with light. As instructed, she knocked on the
unmarked door to the left of the storefront.

A moment later, Jack answered.

"What's the password?" He blocked the doorway
with his arm across the threshold. His biceps strained
against the soft blue cotton sleeves he'd rolled to the elbows.

She held up a paper bag. "Spaghetti marinara from
Cesare's and sangria from my refrigerator."

"Home brew?" He took the bag from her as she entered. "Your mom's recipe?"

"Who else's? You used to have a naughty habit of sneaking a glassful or two from our kitchen way back when."

He shut and locked the door behind her. "And it was worth your sister's wrath when she caught us."

"Caught *us*? Caught you." Angela laughed at the memory, but only briefly. That had been the first incident to put Jack on Kelly's "less than good enough for my little sister" list.

Jack laid the food and drink on an antique oak table that also seemed to serve as a desk. He swept a few near-empty cardboard take-out boxes into the garbage can and stacked several neatly labeled file folders. "Imagine what she'd say if she saw us now."

"I'd rather not." *Play the rest by ear.* Though her sister's words echoed in her mind like a mantra, she knew Kelly never meant her advice to be taken with Jack. "So, you've been working all day without a decent break." Angela noted his appealingly rumpled clothes and the distinctive five o'clock shadow giving his rugged chin a golden hue.

His smile was crooked, like that of an unrepentant child caught with a chocolate-chip cookie just before dinner. "My project was important."

"Oh, what are you working on?"

She half-listened while he outlined the details of the few commitments he had left to finish from projects begun overseas. Her interest was on the converted warehouse. Boxes marked either Personal or Photo Equipment lined the brick walls, painted white to intensify the flow of light into the large space. Except for a loft on the far wall, the place had been gutted.

The space was sparsely furnished with errant desks, tables and boxes. The primary focal point was the room's expansive center, dominated by a tall rigging hooked to several backdrops. Lights, some small, others immense, a few with colored gels, towered like dinosaur skeletons in a museum. Props ranging from a handpainted antique carousel horse to a gleaming Harley-Davidson motorcycle sat on the canvas-covered floor.

She walked over and eyed the Harley more closely. She'd never ridden one, but like most good girls, she had a secret desire to straddle the symbol of ultimate freedom and hit the open road.

"That's a potential prop for my new project." Jack grabbed plastic forks and mismatched souvenir wineglasses from a file cabinet drawer.

"New project? Already? You haven't even settled in."

Damn. Angela had hoped to lure Jack into helping her by offering the challenge of starting his first project at home with an old and trusted friend. Zap Plan A.

"Tell that to my agent. Besides, we made this deal over a year ago, and I have a commitment. My advance paid the bills for the move and the warehouse."

She'd checked the prices of real estate lately. His going rate must be enormous. Though she wasn't offering peanuts, neither was she handing out Godiva-covered macadamias. Scratch Plan B—luring with money.

He had the table set with makeshift appointments, and again, the simple complexity of the man touched her. After the articles she'd read in the rags, she would've bet the bank a man who once dated Lily Dee didn't even know what a paper plate was. She, however, as a single working mother, seriously considered purchasing stock in Chinette.

Jack drew Angela away from a stuffed rack of clothes tucked behind a Japanese screen.

"Do you know how long it's been since I've had Cesare's?" He twisted the top on the glass carafe and poured them each a generous goblet of sangria. "Even in Italy I couldn't find food that good."

Angela shrugged out of her short-sleeved suit jacket and draped it over the back of her chair. "Pasta from Cesare's is a staple at the office when we're pulling an all-nighter." She carefully separated the cardboard covers from the aluminum containers. The heavenly aromas of tomato, garlic and onion wafted up amid the steam. "This is the ultimate comfort food."

She exchanged a serving of spaghetti for a glass of wine.

"I guess I should have brought silverware," she admitted after several failed attempts to get a decent mouthful onto her plastic fork.

With ease, he successfully twisted a generous portion onto his utensil. "Here. I seem to have a flair for it."

Cupping his hand beneath the serving, he offered her his biteful. She considered declining such a personal sacrifice, but the temptation of mouth-watering pasta served by Jack proved irresistible.

She leaned forward, unconsciously licking her lips before he slipped the steaming food onto her tongue. Closing her eyes, she savored the rich flavor as Jack's hands lingered near her mouth.

"How is it?" he asked.

She swallowed with an appreciative sigh. "Words cannot describe the sensation. Let's see if I can show you."

"I love a woman of action."

Their gazes met before she looked away to manipulate the al dente pasta onto her fork. He didn't have a clue how much action he was in for. After capturing a decent helping, she offered the twirled spaghetti.

He took it in a ravenous swallow. "Just as good as I remember." He wiped an errant drop of sauce from the corner of his mouth. "Too bad this isn't finger food, though. We'd have all the makings of an interesting situation."

Though she considered dipping a finger into the red marinara and seeing what they could cook up, she decided otherwise. Business had to come first.

"Well, if our meeting tonight is successful, we could have plenty of opportunities for meals together, fingers and all."

"Meeting? I thought this was just a dinner between friends." His words were innocent. His expression was not.

She ignored his upraised eyebrow and tore open a packet of Parmesan. "It is." She sprinkled cheese on her pasta. "But I have a business situation I need your input on."

He took a sip of wine. "Angela Harris, asking for *my* help? I'm intrigued."

Smirking, she took a swallow of sangria. "I'm self-sufficient, Jack, not stupid. I've learned to utilize my friends' talents to get ahead. They benefit, and so do I."

"And you do know that the two of us working together is a very risky business."

Risky was an understatement. It was downright dangerous.

His words evoked a long-forgotten memory of a time the school newspaper, of which she was editor, and the yearbook, where Jack served as head photographer, tried to work together on a special edition for the school's silver anniversary. While the finished product won numerous local and state awards, the process nearly wrecked their relationship. They both had definite ideas about how and when things should be done. Unfortunately, those notions rarely matched.

Angela couldn't concern herself with whether or not the Davenport project would destroy the tentative connection they'd established. It was better if it did. As long as she won this lucrative account, nothing else mattered.

Did it?

"I don't know. If business progresses as I've planned, we might accomplish two goals at once."

They continued eating dinner while Angela explained Randall's deception and the importance of the Whispering Palms account. Jack listened intently, asked few questions and threw out no accusations or blame. She couldn't help feeling flattered at his assumption that she'd done the best she could for Harris and Associates.

"Every once in a while, the good guys get duped. Happens to the best of us." He punctuated his observation with a hearty mouthful of wine. "But I don't see how I fit in."

"I need a hook." She gathered empty food containers while he refilled their wineglasses. "I have a meeting scheduled with Davenport tomorrow afternoon. I have the pitch in mind, but I need an unusual angle to make it irresistible. I need you as my director of photography."

"I was hoping you needed me for something beyond business."

The tingly effect brought on by the wine emboldened

her. "Maybe I do. Maybe I don't. I prefer to look at this as the perfect opportunity to find out."

His left eyebrow shot up skeptically. "Are you implying that our weekend fling may be more than a weekend fling?"

"Take whatever implication you want, just take my offer, too."

He slid his chair back and downed the last of his sangria before standing. He seemed to be mulling the idea over as he glanced around the studio.

"I foresee a four-color brochure, some slick ads for top architectural magazines, a few thirty-second spots, all featuring your work and highlighting your involvement in the visual design of the homes. Davenport is known for his high-priced condos and multimillion-dollar mansions, but he has a different market to hit with this development."

Jack's eyes began to glaze, so she moved on to her ace in the hole. "Whispering Palms is some of the most gorgeous real estate left in Florida, right down to the nature preserve and wetland bordering one side of the golf course." She paused, knowing she'd intrigued him with the information about the land. Nature shots were his forte. "Of course," she added, "maybe the commercialism of this assignment is too gauche for you. You *are* an artist, after all."

"Don't be ridiculous." He scanned his converted warehouse as if searching for something. "A smart artist knows a solid commercial gig can pay for a hell of a lot of avant garde projects. That assignment I mentioned earlier is for a calendar celebrating scantily clad women and different forms of art. The carousel and the Harley are for the backgrounds."

Angela stood, holding her wineglass. "I understand

the horse—it's obviously hand-carved and painted. But the motorcycle? How is that art?"

"Have you ever ridden one?"

"No," she admitted reluctantly.

"That's why you don't understand."

Angela wandered to the machine and ran her hand over the supple leather seat. The gleaming chrome and metal caught the bright studio lights like icicles with sunshine.

"Care to educate me?"

She turned just in time to catch the blooming of his suggestive smile. "Oh, yes. But not like you think."

6

"JUST WHAT do you have in mind?"

Though casually spoken, her question suggested both fear and curiosity—just as Jack hoped. He took the wineglass from her unsteady hand and set it on the floor beside the bike. As he stood, she crossed her arms over her chest and shifted her weight to one hip—cocked and ready for battle.

Fortunately for him, he had exactly the ammunition he needed.

"I have a challenge for you—a counteroffer I've been obsessing over ever since you called." He dug into her protective self-hug and dislodged her hands. Rhythmically, he worked the tension out of her fingers, then twined her hands with his. "I'm through with one-night stands and weekend flings. Especially with you. This attraction is too strong for that. We need to play it out...in a big way."

"How?" The question popped out quickly, as if she didn't want to give herself too much time to think.

Jack leaned against the seat of the Harley, encouraged by her willingness to hear him out. He wouldn't think about her motivation. He refused to care if she accepted his challenge simply to save her business. His plan would allow him the one thing he needed most—time.

Using her hand as a lifeline, he reeled her closer until

she stood between his parted legs, her thighs against his and her breasts at eye level. "I called you frigid once. I was dead wrong. That I've already learned. But I still don't think you've experienced complete and total passion." He spied the gentle rise and fall beneath the pearlized silk of her blouse and had to bite the inside of his mouth to keep from kissing her there.

"What was Saturday night? Wasn't that passion?"

"With us, there could be so much more."

The idea intrigued her, frightened her. She needed his help, but this wasn't what she'd expected. Or was it?

Instinctively, and despite the proximity between her breasts and his mouth, she assumed the straight-shouldered pose of a practiced negotiator. "Just what kind of challenge do you have in mind?"

His breath skittered across her skin. "When we're alone, like this—" he smoothed his hands over her hips "—you'll do whatever I ask, no matter how unique."

She laughed, but not because his words were funny. The twitter in her voice betrayed her wildly electrified nerves. "Unique? I didn't know you were into kinky."

He shook his head and slid his fingers around her waist. "I'm not. Kinky is for perverts." His body molded to hers like dripping wax to the shaft of a candle. "I simply want to explore every possibility. When we make love again, I want you to be so far over the edge, you'll never forget what I feel like."

The thick desire in his voice and the intense look in his eyes made her swallow deeply, seeking the moisture that abandoned her mouth.

"Will that make you some sort of teacher?"

He took her hand again and placed a gentle kiss on the inside of her wrist, sending a wave of longing through her body. "If you'll let me."

Angela closed her eyes, trying to fight the urge to chew on her bottom lip, trying to ignore the heat rising from his hands along her spine. Her insides dissolved like a poolside Popsicle, the tiny trickles of candy-sweetened juice slithering down her skin, waiting for Jack to lap them with his tongue.

She pushed away, forcing herself to think. His bold offer tugged at her, yet she had to consider his proposal with at least a remnant of logic.

"Don't think, angel," he told her, reading her thoughts. "Just for tonight. Let me show you what I mean. What I want. What I know you want."

He kissed her neck, then disappeared behind a Japanese screen. She heard him rummaging through the rack of lingerie she'd seen there. The quick slide of the metal hanger as he dismissed an outfit reminded her of the measured beat of a snare drum prior to a public hanging.

Don't be dramatic, she told herself. Jack might be planning to take her to the brink of something unknown and terrifying, but he wasn't going to kill her. Unless, of course, she died from embarrassment.

Her fears were nearly confirmed when Jack emerged, dangling three tiny outfits hooked on his index finger.

"Let's see if you're a woman of your word." He approached at a deliberate pace. "You said you were an adventurer. Lesson one is about to begin. If you pass the test, I guarantee you'll win that account."

She took a deep breath, picked up her glass and tossed back the last swallow of wine. The whole situation should have appalled her. The old Angela would have turned on her sensible one-inch heels, but not before slapping Jack squarely across the cheek for suggesting such an exorbitant price. But the new Angela didn't. Deep in the center of her belly, a tremor of excitement began, then slowly, like the vibrations of an earthquake, spread to the rest of her. The mild shaking, partially from fear and partially from anticipation, fired her. The new Angela wanted this as much as he did—maybe even more.

She grabbed the hangers from him.

"Before the bell rings, teach, I want you to understand one thing," she insisted.

"What's that?"

"This student doesn't have a fear of authority. I know how to say no, and when I do, I mean it."

He traced the wispy bangs hanging to her eyebrows, framing her heart-shaped face. Authority sparkled in her hazel eyes, nearly gutting him with need.

"Let's hope you won't have to say no to me. Not ever again."

When she vanished behind the screen, he let out a pent-up breath. If she only knew how much he needed *her* tutelage, she might run screaming out of his life for good.

The sound of her skirt being unzipped set him to work like a starting pistol. She'd accepted the challenge so brazenly, Jack pulled props from boxes with renewed vigor. He searched the mover's manifests as if they were treasure maps and fought the urge to forget the whole thing and simply take her to bed.

As he retrieved his tripod and camera from the area near the carousel horse, he considered Angela's proposal regarding Whispering Palms. She'd disclosed every sordid detail of her associate's betrayal without attempting to evoke pity. Clearly, she blamed herself for not anticipating the jerk's intentions, but not an ounce of angst peppered her tone. Her pragmatism and confidence turned him on—probably a result of the two years he'd spent with Lily.

Remembering that fiasco forced Jack to acknowledge that he would have taken Angela's offer even if she hadn't accepted his sexual challenge. Working with a woman to whom honesty and integrity were more precious than slender hips and unblemished skin could serve to renew the faith he'd once had in women—faith Lily had almost destroyed.

With Angela, he stood a decent chance of finding the one thing that had eluded him all these years—and all his life. Lily's lies made Jack realize, as hokey as it sounded to his own jaded ears, that he wanted a life partner, a wife, perhaps even a family. Who better to start one with than his sweet angel?

Angela's voice from the other side of the screen zapped Lily out of his mind.

"It's kind of quiet in here. Do you have any music?"

He tried not to hear the gentle rustle of material sliding up her skin.

"Any requests?"

She poked her head around the screen. The sight of her bare shoulder caused a pleasant tightening just below his stomach. Was *sweet* the word he had used to describe Angela? Sweet as in the richest dark chocolate.

"You claim to know what I'll like," she purred.

Not exactly, but I'm about to find out. "Barbieri or Kenny G?" he asked, hoping his memory of her preference for brass and jazz proved accurate.

"Either. Both."

She disappeared behind the screen, sending him straight to the CD rack. *Either. Both.* He only hoped she'd hold on to that sentiment once the lights went out and they went to work.

SHE WATCHED the shiny silver zipper in the mirror as she slid it up her back, enclosing herself in snug black leather from just below her buttocks to the top of her neck. Designed like a cycler's sleeveless training suit, the outfit hugged every curve, allowing only glimpses of bare flesh through carefully placed slashes in the fabric. A sewn-in bra lifted her breasts to an enticing peak, and the color slimmed her hips beyond her wildest dreams. She accented the look with lace hose and spiked ankle boots. The designer labels in everything didn't surprise her. Jack Sullivan's tastes didn't run cheap.

He'd handed her three choices, but this one drew her interest as much as the Harley. She was taking her walk on the wild side with a relish that made her laugh. She wrapped a thick sterling chain of tiny linked handcuffs around her wrist.

Some good girl you are.

Sitting on a low stool in front of a brightly lit mirror, she poked around in the drawers for a dark shade of lipstick, forbidding herself to acknowledge any reservations. She'd reviewed all her qualms before she arrived. She knew if he accepted her job offer, they'd make love again. It seemed inevitable. And harrowing. And invigorating. Despite her mixed feelings, she blazed forward.

One lonely night away from Jack convinced her he'd been right. What they'd shared at the reunion was wonderful—but incomplete. Like a bite of forbidden fruit, she needed more. She had to satiate herself with Jack until every question, every possibility was explored and laid to rest. Only then could she leave him and his memory behind.

As she heard the opening bars of a Gato Barbieri

tune, the studio's lights dimmed. The lead-in, a string bass humming softly, lured her from the safety of the dressing area. Cocky in her top-notch leather, she pulled on fingerless gloves.

The studio lights pointed directly at her and shielded Jack from clear view. Behind his tripod, he fiddled with his camera until he sensed her presence. With a few strokes of the control board, the harsh light dissolved into a golden glow. Darkness surrounded them, muting the entire studio as if nothing existed beyond the small space they occupied.

"There isn't film in that camera, is there?" She tried to mask the fearful urgency in her voice. She'd play Jack's game willingly, but she wasn't so certain she wanted tangible proof.

"There might be. That isn't the point." He spoke from the shadows behind the camera.

She placed her hands on her hips. "It damn well ought to be the point if you decide to pass pictures around at our next reunion."

Jack emerged from the darkness. He'd untucked his shirt and kicked off his shoes. A small camera was hung around his neck. His expression made her pulse flutter. He'd said he'd push her beyond her limits.

From the look in his eyes, she believed him.

"I would never do anything to humiliate you, angel. At least, not on purpose."

The poignancy of his words hit her hard. Did he know what she knew? Did he realize how his night with her best friend hurt her? Or did he believe she remained unaware of his betrayal? The flash of residual anger dispersed when he ran his hand up her arm.

"What happens here tonight—or any other night we're together—is between you and me. Exclusively."

The last word, spoken when he was close enough for her to smell the tantalizing scent of the sangria they'd shared earlier, erased her reluctance.

"Can you trust me?" he asked.

She searched for signs of deception, but his green irises, his dilated pupils and the crinkles at the corners of his eyes testified to his sincerity.

"I want to, Jack."

He took her hand in his. "After tonight, you'll *know* you can." He raised her wrist to his lips and tenderly kissed her pulse at the edge of her glove. "I hurt you in the past, angel. I won't again. That's a promise I made to me...and now to you. I won't break it."

She took in his voice and how his words, edged with sensual promise, brimmed with honesty. She forced herself to acknowledge that none of the pain Jack had caused her had come from lies, but from omissions of truth.

"I want to believe you, Jack."

"If you don't," Jack said, his lips searing her temple with a brief kiss, "this won't work. You won't feel what you need to feel—what I know you *want* to feel."

She wanted to feel sexy, desired, free—all the things she'd never had the time or desire to experience until two nights ago. She suspected their first nights together were only a sizzling sparkler compared to the fireworks he promised. In her entire life, no man had tempted her to release her iron grip on the unwritten rules of propriety and decorum.

Except Jack Sullivan.

Still holding her hand, he led her to the Harley, braced upright by clamps around the wheels. The strains of the music broke into her mind and soothed her. Without prompting, she swung her leg over the

seat, then watched with surprise at the darkening of
Jack's eyes and the slight flushing of his skin.

"I bet you look at all your models like that." She
crossed her arms defiantly. Jealousy suddenly bit at her,
giving her cause to cool the molten warmth pooling
within her. The feeling unnerved her. And they hadn't
even started.

"You're unlike any of the models I've ever worked
with, angel. And I've worked with loads of them. But
we're not here to take pictures of a pretty face or create
an illusion for some magazine." He reached under her
thigh and guided her leg across the length of the bike,
chafing the lace against her skin so her nerve endings
flared with sensitivity. "What we're about to do will be
real. This isn't just a fantasy."

"The question is, will it be mine, or yours?" She
stretched forward to wrap her fingers around the hand-
grips and turn them, as if revving the engine.

Angela couldn't deny the fact that though they
wanted each other, their ultimate goals were as dissim-
ilar as the leather and lace she wore. She wanted an affair to end all affairs—a fire hot enough to burn Jack
right out of her life. He wanted a flame that would
brand him right into her soul.

"We're not so different," Jack said, as if sensing her
thoughts. "By the end of the night, you're going to see
how alike we are. How we both want exactly the same
thing."

She let the words swirl in her mind, hoping, if only
for an instant, that Jack would prove himself right.

The music washed over her like a summer storm.
Leaning back, she braced her hands beneath her for balance.

"Okay. Now what?"

She had eased onto the machine without reserve, without any of the protest or shock he had expected. She'd tempted him with her sensual talents at the reunion, but Jack had expected her to revert to her virtuous self at the first sight of black leather and a fully loaded hog. But as she lay there, her buttocks shifting against the oiled seat and the leather straining against her full breasts, Jack forgot the Angela he once knew. And his camera. And his plan. All he could think of was the increasing throb in his groin.

He combed his hand through his hair and swallowed before speaking. "Just relax." He moved to a safer distance. If he stayed close, the temptation to explore the differences between the suppleness of the leather and that of her skin would prove irresistible.

"How does the bike feel?" he asked.

"Cold." She ran her ankle across the handlebars, as if inviting the frigid metal to chill her through her lacy black stockings.

"Let's see if we can't warm it up," he suggested, already feeling the rise in his temperature.

She turned toward him slowly, seductively, knowing he watched her with the eye of an artist and the desire of a man. Jack obviously intended his experiment in passion to focus solely on her—at least, theoretically. Angela had other ideas.

"Is that what we're here to do? Heat up a mass of metal?"

He adjusted the lights, moving them closer so their glow gilded her skin.

"We're here to heat you up," he crooned, his voice clearly meant to seduce her with its honeyed tone. "And to see what it would feel like to have sex on a bike."

"Are we going to have sex on this bike?" She lifted her other leg until she lay on the cycle as if it was a cushioned chaise longue. The question, direct though it was, was important. Angela liked to know what to expect. Surprises rattled her. Even pleasant ones.

"Do you want to?" He'd closed the distance between them again. He probably stood only a few steps away. She'd closed her eyes to block out the glare of the studio lights and she didn't have the audacity to open them yet.

She concentrated on her precarious balance on the motorcycle, which drew her attention to the sensual feel of the powerful machine beneath her.

How fast would it go? How loud would it be?

"I have to admit, I find the idea...titillating," she answered, inherently aware of the similarities between the bike and passionate lovemaking.

"Do you?" he asked, the question accompanied by the first whir and click of his camera. "An interesting word, titillating. Turn toward me."

His first instruction seemed innocent enough, but she tried to prolong the process, attempting to latch onto the brazen seductress she'd discovered within herself for the reunion. With Jack standing so near she could smell the faint fragrance of his cologne, it wasn't hard. The scent of him, the memory of his rock-hard muscles pressed against her heated skin, were like an incantation transforming her into a sexy, uninhibited siren. And she liked the feeling.

The sound of leather rubbing against leather as she adjusted her position contrasted with the sultry sounds of the jazz purring from the speakers. The music, low so as not to block out their voices, gave rhythm to her motion and tempo to the slide of her hand across the chrome exhaust.

"You didn't answer my question." She opened her eyelids slowly. When his flash popped white, she blinked.

"Wouldn't you rather wonder? What would having sex on the bike be like? What would I do?"

She smiled slyly. "Why don't you just show me?"

"No." The word resounded in cacophonic contrast to the velvety jazz.

Her eyes opened wider.

"I'm not going to show you. Not yet," he promised. "I want you to show me."

Balanced on her back, her spiked heels on the handlebars, Angela slid forward and ran her hands down her thighs. She bent and raised her knees above her hips, then wiggled her bottom until she achieved a comfortable position. The attendant tingle brought a sigh to her lips.

A quick glance over her shoulder and the echo of the camera motor told her he'd gone behind his tiny box. How convenient for him to hide when she lay so exposed, so deliciously available. The lace, slightly rough against her skin, pricked her as she stretched. When she slipped her bottom nearly off the seat onto the gas tank, the lingerie caressed her, enticed her, aroused her. Trickles of sweat, beading between her breasts under the hot lights and snug leather, tickled as they traced a path downward.

"Raise your arms over your head," Jack said. Then he asked, "What are you thinking?"

She did as he instructed, arching her back so her breasts were thrust forward. "I'm thinking about the hot lights."

"Is that all?" The camera continued to buzz. The sound grew louder as Jack neared.

She ran her fingers into her hair and shook the tresses until they floated around her in a thick mass of waves.

"No. I'm thinking about how this leather is making me slick and wet."

"How wet?"

He stood directly over her, his hips level with her head.

"Wet enough to slide right off this bike if I'm not careful."

Without taking the camera from his eye, he circled her, snapping shots at close range.

"How does the leather feel against your breasts?"

She closed her eyes, willing herself not to be shocked by the question, only to search for the answer. His words alone caused her to pucker taut and round.

"Tight."

"Feel with your hands. Touch yourself." Before she could protest, he commanded. "Do it. Show me how I'd touch you."

He stood across from her, watching her from behind the handlebars. Poised above her knees, he lowered the camera for an instant until she drew her hands to her breasts, at first cupping them, wishing the neckline was low instead of constraining. Then she circled the tips of her nipples, tracing her areolas, exploring the sensation.

Fingers weren't enough—unless they were Jack's.

"I want this off." She reached to undo the zipper, but it caught, refusing to slide down.

A moment of silence passed before Jack recognized the raw need in her expression. He had no intention of making love to her on the cycle, no matter how deeply he burned for her. They were rekindling the flame, producing a few dangerous flashpoints. But making love again so soon could ultimately douse the fire. He had every intention of leaving her tonight with a terrible ache—one only he could soothe.

"Undo the zipper, Jack."

He let the camera dangle from his neck, the hot lights only partially responsible for the sheen of moisture covering his palms. She'd gone further than he'd imagined, trusting him in this fantasy and playing the part.

"I have a better idea." He knew he'd chosen this lingerie designer's work for a good reason. Pressing two fingers into one of the tears in the leather, he pulled down, widening the gap, revealing the swelled curve of her left breast.

She looked at him with wide-eyed intrigue, then hooked her fingers into a tear at the base of her throat. "I hope this wasn't too expensive."

"It's worth the price," he answered, his throat parched.

She yanked the material slowly, sitting up gradually as her fingers revealed more of her skin. She slipped both hands into a tear at her belly and pulled until he could see the dark curls at the base of her thighs.

He caught her every movement, her every expression on camera.

She took her fingernails to her hose, raising the lace and tearing upward until slashes of pale skin peeked through the black weave. Each rip enraptured her, each movement freed her, urging her toward a naked need that had little to do with the absence of clothing.

Jack whipped the camera off his neck and mounted the bike with her, facing her. He grabbed her hips and pressed them to the swelling beneath his jeans, knowing only that he had to feel her there against him, wanting him.

Angela thrust her fingers into his hair and pressed his lips to hers. The kiss, as hard and hot as the leather seat of the Harley, sapped her breath. She heaved when he pulled back, slipped his hands into the leather and ripped the rest of the top away until her breasts fell free. He grabbed her thighs and wrapped her legs around his waist, lifting her so his mouth could ravage her.

He sucked thirstily, then bit her hard enough to send explosions of color into her eyes but lightly enough for her to cry out with pleasure.

"Oh, yes, yes."

He raised his eyes from his feast and caught her stare.

"Jack, I want you."

The aching between her legs, intensified by Jack's thick sex against her inner thighs, grew until she writhed against him uncontrollably. She couldn't stand the wild sensation. She had to have him. Here. Now.

Visibly winded, Jack pulled her forward and kissed her deeply, their tongues crashing and dueling as desire engulfed them. He lifted her, her legs locked around him, off the bike, then loosened her grip until she stood.

Then he pushed her away.

"Enough."

Dazed, she took two steps back, nearly tripping over the bike.

"What?"

"Please understand. This can't happen. Not tonight."

He stalked to the tripod and slammed his fist against the control board, bringing up the studio lights with an explosive flash.

"What more do you want from me, Jack? I played

your game. I even enjoyed it." She grabbed the torn straps of leather and held them across her chest.

He stepped forward but kept his distance.

"But do you want it to end?"

"What are you talking about?"

"You're too important to me. If we make love now, if we give in, we'll finish what we've only begun to start. Tonight was hot, angel. If I don't get into an icy shower in about ten seconds you're going to find yourself flung to the floor. But this is just the beginning of what we can do together. Just the beginning."

She struggled to understand. Her body screamed in protest.

"Don't you want more?" he asked, though his question seemed more like a plea.

No, she didn't. She didn't want to. And yet, she did. She wanted him with a desperation she'd never experienced. Thoughts of seduction and removing Jack from her system forever disappeared under the fiery need coursing through her veins.

But she did understand him—somewhat. Despite the discomfort and distress assaulting her, she'd experienced blinding passion only moments before. She craved the sensations again, wanted to ingrain them in her memory so she'd never forget how it felt to be a sexually powerful woman.

Silence surrounded her until she gained the ability to nod.

With that, he turned and headed up the staircase lining the outer wall. He left her standing there, confusion on her face and ragged leather and lace hanging from her body.

7

JACK BRACED HIMSELF against the windowpane, watching Angela climb into her Pathfinder with a slam of her car door and speed out of his parking lot with a squeal of tires. After tearing off his shirt, he shoved off his jeans, groaning as the denim strained over his swollen sex. He couldn't get in the shower fast enough, though he knew the cold water couldn't ease his discomfort.

As the water pelted him, he called himself a fool. He'd schemed to bring Angela to the brink of a passion so different and erotic she'd yearn for him with an insuppressible hunger—one that would take more than one night to satisfy. But his plan backfired with the force of a Mack truck. The brunt of the blast had pummeled him senseless.

He'd wanted Angela for ten long years. Only two nights ago, he'd made love to her, though it seemed like a century since he'd felt himself inside her, surrounded by her, penetrating the walls she'd built around her body and soul. He'd kept himself from ravishing her downstairs by focusing on the future—by reminding himself he wanted her for more than a night, a week or even a month. But what a night it would have been.

He stood in the shower stall for nearly half an hour, wishing he was in England where the tap ran cold as ice, instead of Florida, where the tepid water barely eased the ache between his legs. He almost resorted to other means, but resisted. He'd wait for her. A few more days wouldn't kill him. He considered hiding his car keys to avoid a late-night visit to her home, then he realized he didn't know where she lived.

He toweled himself quickly, wrapped the terry cloth around his waist and turned off the downstairs studio lights from the upstairs switch. He didn't glance over the railing, knowing one glimpse of the Harley would torture him as much as his memory of Angela in torn leather and shredded lace. In the darkness, he went downstairs, locked the door, then returned to the loft with lightning speed.

Coward. He flung off the towel, pulled on the loosest pair of boxers he could find and fell onto his bed, knowing sleep wouldn't come. Maybe if he focused on her business proposition, he wouldn't fixate on the way she'd thrust her breasts into his mouth, or the sweet taste of her nipples between his teeth, or the demanding plunge of her tongue against his.

Though he'd been out of the States for a while, he knew the reputation Davenport Homes held in the upscale housing market. Angela mentioned the Whispering Palms development near Orlando, but Davenport operated in nearly every state from his main base in California to the condo market in New York. One of Jack's sisters lived in a Davenport home, but which sister he wasn't sure. Thanks to parents who viewed marriage and family as a revolving door, Jack had half a dozen sisters and two brothers scattered around the world. Except for his older sister Jenna, the child who caused his parents to marry in the first place, he had little contact with them. And he only saw Jenna because she'd spent the last five years as a fashion coordinator for a top magazine. If they hadn't crossed paths doing business, Jack doubted he'd see her at all.

But what did he expect from his bizarre family? He slid under the crisp cotton sheet and stared at the ceiling, remembering when Linda and Sully divorced. Jack had only been six years old, but he still associated a sigh of relief with the moment his mother's lawyer brought the papers for her signature.

The feeling ended when his mother married the lawyer the next year, only to divorce him before Jack graduated elementary school. After that, he'd witnessed her parade of stepfathers and "uncles" with detached disgust. He resigned himself early on to the belief that he'd turn out the same way—unable to commit to anyone and unwilling to believe in love—until he met Angela.

Drama class brought them together, and the fact that her family operated with similar craziness gave them a common bond. Though her parents remained married and faithful, they traveled extensively with their business, leaving their two daughters to fend for themselves. Remarkably, Angela subscribed to a deep belief in the importance of family. Once or twice, she'd broken through Jack's teenage cynicism. He'd let himself dream about lasting love—until excessive adolescent testosterone kicked the romantic notion right out of his head.

Now he was older, wiser and more cynical than ever. He yearned to have Angela restore his battered faith in love, marriage and family—ideals he'd tried to find with Lily, though he should have known from the start this pursuit would fail. Lily may have come from a big family reared in a medium-size midwestern city, but the stars of fame sparkled in her eyes like the lights of

Paris. Even when he suspected their relationship would fail, he'd never imagined the circumstances.

They'd been doing a location shoot in Dublin when Lily became ill, queasy and pale as if from a mysterious stomach virus that lasted a few weeks. Then, after a discreet trip to the doctor and a quick sojourn to London, she'd returned as beautiful as ever—and twice as cold. And since rumors moved swiftly in the fashion industry, he learned the reason she'd left Ireland so swiftly and returned with such bitterness.

Jack rolled over, groaning, trying to forget how Lily had refused to answer his pointed questions. She told him not to worry about it. He told her to leave. Before she'd finished packing, he'd received his invitation to the reunion. Sweet memories of his Angela and the possibility of a new life propelled him out of the rented flat in less than three days.

Maybe he'd been foolish. Maybe he'd been idealistic and desperate. But seeing Angela again, even with her newfound sensuality, injected him with the impetus he needed. Now he had a chance to extend their time together and make up for his past sins. She hadn't said as much, but Jack knew that without the Davenport account, Angela might lose Harris and Associates.

The prospect of helping her—really helping her—lightened his brooding mood. She hadn't asked him to prove anything to her. She seemed to hand over her trust with an ease that amazed him, given the countless reasons he'd given her to doubt him. At barely eighteen, he'd been stupid to toss her aside because she wouldn't give in to his sexual advances. Of course, what he'd done afterward was worse.

Jack kicked the sheets off and threw his arm over his eyes. The memory of the post-prom party was hazy, at best, yet he distinctly remembered waking up in the back seat of his car at dawn, half-dressed, with Angela's best friend, Chryssie, draped over his lap. He'd been too drunk to recall in detail what had happened, but he had a damn good idea. If Angela knew how they had betrayed her, breakup or not, he was sure she wouldn't be speaking to him now, much less asking him to help her on the most important business project of her career.

Jack rolled over, shoved a pillow under his head and tried to get comfortable. Angela didn't know the whole story, but Jack did have a lot to prove to her—a lot to prove to himself. And he intended to succeed, no matter what it cost.

"HE'S HERE," Nancy's disembodied voice announced over Angela's office intercom.

She slapped the call button, not caring that he'd hear her instructions. "Make him wait. Outside, if you can."

Before she'd disengaged the system, the door to her office swung open and Jack slipped inside with Nancy on his heels.

"You've gotta be quicker than that, Ms. Brennan, if you plan to run effective interference."

Angela smiled as Nancy shot Jack the nastiest look her fresh face could muster. "I'm an executive assistant, Mr. Sullivan, not an offensive tackle. Though I wouldn't mind taking up the asinine sport if it gave me the strength to throw you out on your arrogant butt."

Jack drew his hand to his chest as if he'd been wounded. He looked to Angela for sympathy, but got no more than a shrug and a sardonic smile.

"She's lethal, angel. It's no surprise that you hired her."

"Yes, and I'd like to keep her happy so she'll stay. You can go, Nan. I'll be fine. He's annoying, but he's relatively harmless."

Nancy turned on her heel with a defiant spin and gave the door a slam on her way out.

Angela wished what she'd said was true. Jack Sullivan was anything but harmless. She'd learned that the hard way last night. A twinge of heat sparked in the center of her belly at the memory, despite her efforts to stay mad at him and thwart any renewed desire.

"You're early." She closed her laptop and slid it into its case.

Jack plopped into the chair across from her desk. The sound of his slacks against the leather sounded uncomfortably familiar.

"I didn't want to deal with traffic. I-4 is a bear with all the construction."

His attempt at chitchat drew a twisted smirk.

"Let me get the finished proposal from Nancy and we can go."

Angela headed for the door, hoping for a moment of refuge prior to being locked up in the car with him for two hours. She hadn't spoken to him since he'd left her, wanting, aching, last night. She'd stood alone in the studio, looking ridiculous and feeling humiliated, until she became angry enough—at him and herself—to rip off what remained of the leather bodysuit and throw on her clothes. Driving home at a legal speed took all her self-control. Only a late-night swim in her pool calmed her enough to sleep. And damned if her dreams weren't haunted by glittering chrome Harleys and slick black leather.

"Not so fast, Angela." Jack shot up and grabbed her wrist before she turned the knob. "We need to talk."

"We have the entire car ride to fill with chatter." She strained slightly against the heat of his skin and the fresh ocean scent of his cologne.

"Now."

He led her to the couch that lined the southern wall of her office.

She sat reluctantly, fighting the urge to reclaim her hand from his. "Look, I understand what happened."

"I wouldn't have left you if I didn't think you understood."

Actually, she had no idea if her suspicions were true or not. Why would a man who claimed to want her so badly, who encouraged her to be more erotically bold and enticing than she'd ever felt before, suddenly push her away? He'd told her from the beginning he didn't want just a one-night stand, but his means to draw their relationship out had to be as torturous to him as they were to her. Why would a man put himself through such punishment? Men simply didn't do that.

Unless they are in love.

Angela shoved the thought out of her mind. Jack Sullivan had had his chance to love her. And he blew it. Besides, he didn't believe the emotion existed, and she couldn't afford to entertain the notion that he'd changed his mind—not with Dani in her life.

The more time she spent with him, the more she worried about the condition of her heart. She'd thought he remained in her dreams for all these years simply because she hadn't slept with him. Now she wasn't so sure.

"I've accepted your challenge, Jack. It wasn't easy last night. I can't deny that. But if we're going to go through with this, then we both have to face hard choices. There's nothing left to discuss."

He took her chin in his hand, examining her face closely. "You sound so serious, as if our relationship is just another business deal."

She jerked her face away. "I'm sorry." She stood, walked to the door and clutched the knob fiercely. "Look, I'm riding a caffeine high, I'm nervous about this meeting, and the last thing I need to deal with right now is what happened last night. That woman on the Harley can't pull off this deal."

Jack made no move to join her. "You are that woman on the Harley."

She left, not allowing herself to consider whether or not he was right. Luckily, he let the subject drop once she'd gathered the proposals from Nancy and handed him a large portfolio case.

As he pushed open the tinted glass doors of her office building, the sunlight blinded her. Her eyes adjusted as he stepped around her and popped open the trunk of his car.

She couldn't suppress a grin. The man was inventive. "A white Mustang convertible?"

He placed the portfolio in the trunk, slammed the lid closed and unlocked and opened the passenger door. "I can see the effect I intended isn't lost on you."

He didn't miss a beat. She'd reminded him about the car only four nights ago.

She slipped past him and ducked into the car. "I get the joke, Jack."

He leaned in and reached across to insert her seat belt buckle into the lock. "It's no joke, angel. You said you might want to test out the back seat, remember?"

"Is that what I said?"

His green eyes danced with promised delight.

"Well, not this afternoon," she insisted. "We have a major client to win over first."

Jack slammed the door and jogged to the driver's side, then slid into the seat with virile grace. "Agreed. But once we've succeeded, we'll need to celebrate."

He started the engine without further comment, but an expectant grin tilted the corners of his mouth.

Angela set her lips in a determined smile. There was no telling what could happen later. Revenge could, she reminded herself, be deliciously sweet.

THE MEETING progressed without a hitch, and by the time they'd finished dessert at the Whispering Palms' brand-new, and not yet open, restaurant, Angela had a signed contract in her briefcase and an ecstatic client pouring her a glass of brandy. She hadn't known Davenport owned two of Jack's prints in his private collection or that he'd followed the work of Jack's sculptor father, Sully Sullivan, for years. Still, she let Davenport suspect she had nosy little spies crawling through the woodwork. The idea that she went to such lengths to secure his business delighted the man. And who was she to stop any male from catching a good thrill?

With dinner over and plans to meet with Davenport's design team and take a preliminary round of photos the following day, Jack wordlessly escorted Angela to the car. Yet, by the way he caressed her arm as he helped her inside, she suspected they'd be spending the evening together.

Sunset shadowed the sky with lavender hues as Jack pulled out of the parking lot. The summer evening air remained thick with heat and swollen with possibilities. The trill of her cellular phone saved her from imagining what those possibilities might be.

"Angela Harris."

"Ange, it's Kelly." Her sister's voice seemed rushed, as if worried.

Turning her shoulders, Angela fruitlessly attempted to gain some privacy. "Kell, what's wrong?"

"Nothing major. The boys just called from camp. It's been raining for four days, and they're begging to come home."

Angela let out a pent-up breath. Her nephews, as much as she adored them, weren't the "roughing it" types and hadn't taken to the idea of summer camp as readily as Dani had. They'd find any excuse to leave the rustic mountain retreat and return to their backyard pool and cable television.

"Did you talk to the counselors? Is the weather dangerous?"

She'd watched the weather channel this morning, and there had been no mention of flooding in the area of the camp.

"A few of the creeks are swollen," Kelly replied, "but they expect the weather to lighten up tomorrow. Still, Garrett isn't too keen on paying all this money if the kids are miserable. We're going to drive up tomorrow and get them. I just wanted to know if you wanted me to get Dani, too."

The name, spoken in Jack's presence even if she knew he couldn't hear, caused an uncomfortable tremor in her stomach. "Did you talk to her?"

"The boys did. They said she wants to stay. I told them to have her call you at eight-thirty. I knew you'd be back from your meeting by then."

Angela glanced at her watch. It was nearly seven-fifteen. If they hurried, and made no stops, she'd make it home in time to receive the call. Dani could contact her on the cellular phone—she had the number and knew to use it if the line at home went unanswered. However, the last thing she wanted was to talk to her daughter with Jack around. He didn't know anything about Dani, and she intended to keep it that way.

"We're on our way to the office now. I'll come right over, okay?"

"We?" Kelly inquired, her voice lilting with curiosity.

"I'll be home in an hour, Kell."

Angela pressed the end button and slipped the phone into her briefcase. She'd hidden her association with Jack from Kelly the same way she'd concealed Dani's existence from Jack. Her sister would be livid to learn Jack was in her life, even if only for business. And there was no telling how Jack would react to learning he might have fathered a daughter during a drunken one-night stand with her best friend and that Angela had raised her for the past four years. She rubbed her temples in tiny circles, trying to dispel an impending headache.

"Anything wrong?" Jack wondered as he eased the car onto the main road outside the subdivision.

Angela jumped, unaware that Jack had turned his concerned gaze from the road and trained it on her. She sat back in the seat and fiddled with the seat belt. "That was Kelly. Seems my nephews have had enough of summer camp, and she's leaving first thing in the morning to pick them up. She needs me to come over by eight-thirty to help her get some things together."

Jack nodded, but the corners of his mouth dipped into a frown.

So much for the back seat.

"You look disappointed," she purred, feeling safe enough as he accelerated the car onto the interstate to slide her briefcase behind her and lean across the console until her lips were less than an inch from his ear. "Did you have another challenge for me tonight, Jack?"

He threw the car into a higher gear.

Tracing the edge of his ear with featherlight fingertips, she licked his lobe and whispered, "You did, didn't you?"

"I'm driving," he pointed out, his voice betraying a hint of discomfort. He shifted in his seat.

She smiled. Paybacks were hell.

"And you do it so very, very well."

She ran her palm down his arm, then closed her hand around his as he gripped the gearshift. "You hold it so tight." She licked her lips slowly, making sure he caught her movement in his peripheral vision. "You're giving me ideas."

"If you want to arrive at your sister's in a hurry, you'd better not entertain them," he warned.

She moved closer, twisted out of the shoulder harness and nipped at his neck with her teeth. "Oh, come on, Jack. You're a talented guy. You can do two things at once."

"What two things?"

The question seemed ridiculous, as if she should know better than to tease a man mercilessly while he maneuvered a powerful sports car down a major highway. She did know better, so she'd be careful not to distract him too much—just enough to make him pay for leaving her so unsatisfied the night before.

"I was pretty mad at you last night." She loosened his tie and slid the silk from around his collar. She undid the top button of his shirt and watched his Adam's apple bob when he swallowed. "But the way you dazzled

Davenport until he was practically eating out of your hand really turned me on."

"Is that so?"

She fanned herself with her hand. "You made me hot."

Returning to her seat, she flicked on the radio and tuned it to an oldies rock station. His sigh of relief was short-lived. She shrugged out of her suit jacket and tossed it on the back seat. The gold silk shell she wore beneath her forest green suit was nearly transparent, and she wore no bra.

You are that woman on the Harley, she reminded herself.

"Real hot."

She toggled the air conditioner higher. She kicked off her shoes and eased her seat back. Her short skirt hiked slightly up her thighs.

"Angela, you're asking for trouble."

Languidly, she placed her right hand behind her head and relaxed in the seat.

"I'm cooling off, Jack. That's the only safe alternative, right? I don't have time for trouble. I have to get home."

He glanced away from the road for an instant, groaned, then turned his gaze to the gray line of highway ahead of him.

"You're about to cause an accident."

Jack's knuckles cramped as he clutched the steering wheel tighter. Twilight descended like a plum-colored curtain, and the traffic ahead blinked at him with tiny red lights. Red meant stop. Didn't she see them? Here he was, trying to be considerate, and this is how she repaid him? Despite all they'd been through in the past few days, she didn't even begin to understand the complexity of his desire for her. Hell, he didn't, either. But with the pace of his growing need, she'd better back off before he yanked the car off the road and pulled her into his uninitiated back seat.

"You know," she continued, her voice deliberately raspy and deep, "I wonder what sex in a moving car is like." She leaned sideways, allowing her draping blouse to reveal the pale curve of her breast. "Think you could keep the car on the road?"

At that, Jack swung the car onto the shoulder, jamming on the brakes and forcing Angela to brace her hands on the dashboard to keep from flying forward. When the car stopped, he threw it into park and pulled up the emergency brake with such force, he thought he'd ripped it off.

She reached behind, grabbed her jacket and draped it over her legs like a lap blanket.

"Modest all of a sudden?" He shook his head at her shyness. Maybe she did understand the danger of the fire she toyed with.

She glanced at him with a sidelong, stabbing glare. "You wouldn't know much about modesty, would you?"

"Judging from the way you play highway harlot, you aren't exactly Miss Manners either, sweetheart."

Ouch. Yet he couldn't help his scathing response. The holier-than-thou tone in her voice could cause a saint to lose his temper. And Jack was no saint.

"No, Miss Manners I'm not. I guess any high-powered road vehicle brings out the worst in me."

The admission seemed resigned and nearly as weary as the look in her eyes. Jack grinned inwardly. She still smarted from last night. This had been her attempt at revenge. Clever. And almost successful.

"Not the worst, the best. And I'm sorry about the

Miss Manners crack. What happened between us deserves better."

His apology did nothing to soften the spite in her stare. "Why? Because we're meant for each other? Because we're in *love?*"

The last word came out long, with a melody of sarcasm—sarcasm that usually came from him. The sound, emanating from Angela's sweet lips, was raucous and raw. He ached to hold her in his arms and kiss her until he took the sound away, but he sensed the futility. A kiss wouldn't be enough. Sex wouldn't be enough.

Unfortunately, they were all he had to give. What was missing had to come from her.

"No, we're not in love. But the possibility exists."

She scoffed. "You don't have to sweeten the deal with empty promises, Jack. I don't expect or want us to fall in love."

Silence reigned for a moment, and he could feel her stare. He turned off the ignition and adjusted the rearview mirror—anything to keep from hurting. He'd prepared himself for her anger over last night, but what he sensed now was deeper, more embittered.

He kept his gaze glued to the darkening road. "Not even you always get what you want, angel."

"You don't really believe you're going to fall in love with me? I mean, that's not like you."

"That's not like the old me," he said, unable to remove the frustration from his voice. "I keep trying to show you I've changed." *I keep trying to show myself.*

"Is that what you've been doing? And I thought you were awakening my most secret hidden passions."

Her mocking tone severed his control like a knife slice to a taut rope. She turned to continue her tirade, but he stopped her with a hand across her mouth.

"Don't, Angela. Don't say one more word."

A series of quick emotions flashed in her eyes—anger, fear, then bitter resignation. He removed his hand and leaned back in his seat, gripping the steering wheel until his knuckles whitened.

"I don't know how else to show you I've changed. I'm not the callous boy I used to be. And if I've awakened your most secret hidden passions, it was because you wanted them awakened. By me."

She turned her face away, and he could only see her silhouetted reflection in the window from the dim dashboard light. She'd picked a fight with him purposefully, as if to destroy the magnetic emotions drawing them closer together. He should have expected this. She was afraid of what they shared.

So was he.

Suddenly, he felt very tired. He glanced at his watch, calculating the short distance they'd traveled in comparison to how far they still had to go. "We don't have to talk now."

"We don't have to talk ever. We just need to finish this deal and say goodbye."

Taking several lung-filling breaths, Jack eased the car back onto the road and set the cruise control at a safe and even speed. He didn't answer her. He didn't know how. He didn't even know which deal she referred to.

He was suddenly glad he'd made this trip to Tampa so many times before, because for the time being, anyway, he had no idea where he was going.

8

ANGELA TOSSED her unfinished crossword into the garbage and peeked into her coffee mug. Two or three swallows remained, but she blanched at the thought of drinking them. The caffeine she'd already consumed had her nerves rattled enough without another cupful to put her over the edge.

She stacked her late-lunch plates in the dishwasher and wiped the already clean table. She searched the house for something to dust, vacuum or polish. Funny how the house remained pristine when Dani was away.

Funny how much she hated it.

Before Dani came to live with her, Angela had been a certifiable neat-freak. She could still remember with perfect vividness the first time Dani had spilled grape juice on her carpet, only a week after she'd moved in. The stain had meant nothing. All she'd cared about was soothing away the terrified expression on her daughter's face, returning the twinkle to her pixie green eyes.

Angela slid onto the couch and scooped up a marketing journal she hadn't had time to read, trying to ease the ache the memory created. Never in her life did she think she could love someone as deeply as she loved Dani. Her parents traveled so much, Angela understood they didn't love her or her sister with such intensity. Only when she'd seen Kelly with her boys had Angela hoped for the same kind of connection to a child. Then she had Dani. She missed her like crazy.

She appreciated the comfort of her stretchy biker shorts and floppy T-shirt after spending the day before trapped in high heels and a business suit. She'd managed to wine and dine three major clients with lunch, cocktail and dinner appointments, each scheduled around meetings with other local customers of Harris and Associates.

In the end, she'd accomplished two goals. First, she'd reassured most of her temperamental clientele that she and her company were still on top and more than willing to meet their marketing and promotional needs. Second, she'd gone through an entire day without thinking about Jack.

Today, she couldn't get him off her mind.

She hated to admit she missed him. Since last Friday night, they'd been together nearly every day. Whether for business or pleasure, their encounters always proved exhilarating, fresh and sometimes even oddly comfortable. Except for the drive back from the meeting with Davenport. What had started out as a teasing act of revenge ended in a bitter battle of emotions.

She didn't quite know exactly what had caused her feelings to turn so quickly to resentment. His wisecrack about her lack of modesty, an observation richly deserved, wasn't the culprit. Something deeper was to blame. Something simpler.

Fear. Her fear.

Without uttering a complaint, he'd changed his plans for the night to get her home to her sister. Even when her words had slashed at him, he'd shown unwavering patience. In high school, she was neither the first nor the last girl left in the dust when Jack thought things were getting too intense. Now, the intensity sprang from him.

So far as she knew, his longest relationship, a well-publicized tryst with supermodel Lily Dee, ended almost as swiftly as it began. Though Angela tried not to believe everything she read, the gossip mongers implied Jack dumped Lily in lieu of marriage. After her prom night heartbreak, Angela had no trouble buying this story. How far off the truth could the media be when the stories fit so perfectly into his modus operandi?

But what if his m.o. had changed?

She threw the journal on the table, suddenly dissatisfied with staying inside on such a clear summer day. After her work yesterday, few tasks awaited her attention at the office. Nancy was already pouring through portfolios and had set up a meeting with Jack to interview models for the brochure he'd shoot for investors and potential homeowners. If she stayed home, as planned, she'd conveniently miss running into him until tomorrow's strategy session.

Ordinarily, she'd spend this free summer afternoon entertaining her daughter or shopping with her sister. But with Dani at camp and Kelly on her way back from retrieving her sons, Angela faced a rare weekday alone.

She decided to enjoy the sunny weather by the pool. She donned her swimsuit and filled a small cooler with ice and sodas. Once they'd chosen the models and layout designs for the Whispering Palms brochure and magazine advertisements, she'd find no time for relaxation until her and Dani's annual trip to Napa Valley. With two weeks left until their scheduled departure, she had to grab what time for herself she could.

The sun, unhindered by clouds and gleaming strong

despite the late afternoon hour, reminded her to slather on sunscreen before she clicked on the CD player and reclined in her cushioned lounge chair. As the inside of her eyelids swirled with neon yellows, oranges and greens, she attempted to stifle the question running rampant through her mind all morning.

What exactly did Jack want from her?

She turned up the volume on the music. She hummed. She sang. Badly. Nothing worked. As much as she'd tried to evade the inquiry badgering her brain, she couldn't. Why had Jack *really* returned to Florida? A jet-setter like him didn't relocate his internationally known business to a midsize city far removed from New York or Los Angeles without a reason.

People changed. He'd told her he had. He'd shown her. Why couldn't she accept his claim as truth? Was she so afraid of his power over her that she couldn't acknowledge he simply wanted to be with her—if only for a while? Though she'd tried not to see it, Jack Sullivan the teenager and Jack Sullivan the man were definitely not the same.

Without doubt, Jack intended his challenge to be much more than a sexual exploration. He made no secret that he wanted a deeper relationship. She'd blown his words off as a line. Yet, on the way back from Orlando, he'd practically told her he intended to fall in love with her. That wasn't like Jack at all.

He didn't believe in love—at least, that's what he'd told her one night shortly after his mother's marriage to her fourth husband. At the time, his confession made her determined to change his mind. When he left her standing alone on the prom dance floor, she'd realized how foolish she'd been.

So why would he change his mind?

She slid open the top of the cooler and fished out a soda, jumping when an icy drop of water spilled onto her skin. She popped open the top, swallowed a gulp of cola and made a decision. As much as she'd wanted to avoid another intimate confrontation with him, she had to find out where Jack was coming from—and, more important, where he was going. Despite her best efforts, the man simply wouldn't go away easily. She had to know why.

He couldn't know about Dani. Chryssie took the secret of Dani's father's identity to her grave. Even Angela wasn't one-hundred-percent sure about the child's paternity, and she wouldn't be until Jack took a genetic test. His results could be compared with the data Dani's pediatrician gathered during a routine checkup. For this to happen, she'd have to tell Jack of her suspicions.

The thought inspired chills. *No way*. She wouldn't play that hand until Lady Luck deserted her completely. Before Dani came home, Angela had to discover what Jack *really* wanted from her—above and beyond sex and his intimations about love.

With the decision made and the sun blanketing her with its steady heat, she drifted into a semiconscious state between catnapping and dozing. Her ears heard the classical CDs she'd chosen, the birds and squirrels playing tag in her overgrown grapefruit tree and the gentle lapping of the pool water as the mechanical filter wheeled along the bottom. She barely heard the sound of the cooler top dropping to the deck floor. The intrusion didn't register until she heard an aluminum can break free of the packed ice.

She opened her eyes. "What are you doing here?"

Jack smiled and popped open a soda.

"You didn't answer the doorbell. I heard the CD and

walked around back. You should get a dog or something.''

She sat up and wiped the perspiration from her face
with her towel, then let the cloth drop onto her chest,
covering her from his increasingly appreciative gaze.

''How did you get my address?''

Jack slipped his sunglasses on and reclined on the
chaise longue beside hers. Despite the weather, he
looked confidently cool in his light denim shirt and
khaki slacks.

''Nancy. I told her I had some preliminary photographs to show you from yesterday's shoot, and when
she said you wouldn't be in until tomorrow, I insisted I
drop them off. Is this a problem? Are you secretly married or something? Is the hubby about to discover us?''
He attempted to look frightened, but failed. ''You're
looking pale for someone who's spent the afternoon in
the sun.''

He slid his sunglasses down his nose.

''There's no husband.'' She flicked the towel away
and resumed her relaxed position, ignoring her accelerated heartbeat. ''You just startled me.''

''I was hoping I'd be a pleasant surprise,'' he said, his
grin arrogant.

''Fat chance.'' She rolled the towel into a makeshift
pillow and closed her eyes. She needed to talk to him.
Now was the perfect time—dammit. Maybe if she
closed her eyes really tight and concentrated...

''I'm not leaving, Angela. You and I need to talk.''

''No, we don't,'' she insisted, ashamed of herself for
not having more courage. She needed time to prepare.
''We can talk tomorrow, when we're in the office. Right
now, I'd much rather enjoy my afternoon off.''

"What we'll talk about has nothing to do with the office."

She could tell by his voice he'd agreed to forestall their discussion. However, his leaving wasn't part of the deal. She heard him slurp another long sip of cola.

"You can leave the pictures on the table under the gazebo," she added, hoping the dismissal would be clear. Even with her eyes closed, she sensed he'd kicked off his deck shoes.

"I don't think you want these pictures laying around for the yardman to pick up during his beer break."

She sat and turned to face him. "I do the yard myself, thank you. What's so secret about the pictures, anyway? Did you catch some illegal dumping at Whispering Palms?"

"Who said all the pictures were from Whispering Palms?" His devilish smile made her shiver, despite the eighty-degree temperature.

"Jack, those aren't pictures from..."

"Leather suits you. It really does."

A villainous thrill trickled down her spine. She grabbed for the manila envelope, which he efficiently snatched away and hid behind his back.

"Fine." She took a swallow of her sun-warmed soda, then dumped the drink on the nearby grass and shoved the empty can into the cooler. "I don't want to see them. You can destroy them, for all I care."

"My, my," Jack admonished, unfazed by her temper. "You are more and more hostile by the minute. I think you're just too hot, angel. I think you need to cool off."

Despite her best efforts, her body responded to the seductive look in his eyes and the honeyed tone of his voice. The warmth of the sun mingled with a more intimate heat. As if they each possessed a memory of their own, her nerve endings sprung to life, primed and ready for Jack's attention. Even her nipples hardened.

"Jack, I'm not in the mood," she lied. How could she not be when he looked at her with such open desire? No matter the lack of sincerity in other aspects of their relationship, their mutual hunger proved honest. Unreserved. Undeniable.

"Really?" He slid onto her chaise and passed his thumb pads over her taut nipples. "You look ready."

"Looks can be deceiving," she mumbled, but the words died under the pressure of his lips on hers.

He kissed her softly, his thumbs still attending to her breasts with rhythmic, swirling circles. When she gasped his name, he slipped his hands down her slick skin, exploring her exposed ribs and slender waist.

"You're so hot," he said.

"It's July." She tried to reason with him despite his nibbling on her earlobe.

"July or not, I'm going to cool you down." He slid one hand into her swimsuit bottom. His touch trailed over her curled mound and dipped into the folds of flesh at the base. She immediately pooled, wet and ready.

She wanted him. Her mind, filled by need, pushed away every fear, every question, every doubt. They were alone. The hedges of her backyard extended up six feet, providing a private haven. A million other reasons existed for Angela to say no, to insist they not travel this path again. She couldn't think of a single one. She could only surrender to the concentrated fire spreading through her with every stroke of Jack's hands and lave of his tongue.

She unbuttoned his shirt and hungrily ran her hands over his chest, amazed at how familiar he'd become to her. She marveled at the way she knew just how far to spread her fingers until they reached his firm male nipples or how much past his muscled chest lay the tawny hair leading into his waistband. She explored him anew, empowered by his deep-throated groans.

She heard the rustling of ice but still leaped forward when the chill touched her shoulder.

"Relax," he said, "lie back. I told you I'd cool you off."

A drop of icy moisture fell down her shoulder toward her breast. Before the bead disappeared in the material of her swimsuit, Jack lapped it up.

He slipped a cold hand around her neck and undid her top. "We can't have this in the way."

She remained quiescent, her eyes nearly closed, her lips slightly parted, anticipating the next arctic drop.

Starting at the hollow of her neck, he traced the misshapen cube downward. Her flesh puckered in response to the intense cold, then calmed with each scorching kiss. The contrast between the heat surrounding them, the chill of the ice and the warmth of his tongue on her flesh made thought impossible. She could do nothing but feel.

When he reached her left breast, he swirled the ice against her nipple until the coldness pursed her skin with the slightest pain.

She shivered and squirmed, eager to experience the relieving heat of his lips. He waited until her eyes sprang open, then took her full into his mouth and sucked the cold away. Crying out his name, she pushed her hand into his hair, pressing him closer, accepting the breadth of the sensation.

As he bathed her in heat, he touched the ice to her other breast, waiting until she grabbed his cheeks and forced his mouth to warm her freezing skin. Before she could stop him, he'd taken another sliver of ice from the cooler. This time, he slipped the large piece into his mouth.

"What are you doing?" she asked.

His tilted eyebrows promised erotic delight. She couldn't help smiling when he slid her suit off and traced the ice up her ankle, across the back of her knee, up her delicate inner thighs.

His wintry hands guided her legs apart, allowing him full access. The elongated cube, clenched tightly between his teeth, emitted a frosty steam as he hovered above her, allowing a chilly drop to trickle into the sensitive folds.

"Ooh. That feels so..." Another droplet kissed her with cold. "Good."

With the cone-shaped ice, he opened the pleats of flesh, bathing her in dew. His mouth, so near, added the warmth of his breath. When he pushed the ice inside her, she cried out, her mind lost in the shivering. He took the ice in his hand, dipping in and out, in and out, while his tongue lapped the melted moisture.

When the ice disappeared, he used his fingers, restoring the heat lost from the icy droplets. Nearer and nearer the brink of passion came, but the threshold remained far away—too far to be reached with only this. His hands were no longer enough, his mouth only an appetizer. She needed more. She demanded more.

Grabbing his shoulders, she forced him to sit up. She unzipped his pants while locked in a kiss and slid his slacks over his hips.

"I can't stand this." His breath came in spurts. "I have to have you. Now."

"Yes, Jack, yes. I can't think. I just know I want you."

He stood, taking her with him, struggling to rid himself of his pants while she reached into his boxers. She wrapped her fingers around him, thrilling at the length and thickness of him, wanting to feel him deep inside her. The desire, so ingrained, cut to the surface of her heart. She nearly cried at the pain.

"Let's go inside." He stepped back until her shins touched the chaise.

"Yes," she answered, breathless with need and not caring where they made love so long as he didn't pull away again. "Inside."

He wrapped her beach towel around her, draped his slacks, shirt and her swimsuit over his shoulder and lifted Angela into the cradle of his arms. He tucked the manila envelope and his shoes under his elbow.

His irises darkened with lucid desire. "Point me in the direction of heaven, angel."

Bracketing his cheeks with damp palms, she kissed him long and hard, then indicated the door with her foot. Why fight the inevitable? Her body flowed toward Jack like the Mississippi to the gulf. No force of nature could stop that motion any more than her logical mind could keep her from wanting this more than she wanted her next breath.

They moved into the house without parting lips. Knocking over some books and an acrylic picture frame as they crossed into the back hall toward the bedroom, they laughed and showered each other's faces in featherlight kisses. The passion cooled to a steady simmer, ready to be stoked to a burning heat in the privacy of her bedroom.

Jack let her down slowly, allowing her bare legs and towel-wrapped body to slide down every measure of his. He dropped their clothes to the floor, but not before extracting a foil square from his pocket. Unlike their first encounter, where he'd attempted to take it slow but couldn't, Angela could see Jack was in no hurry. Angela helped him slip on the condom. Images of Harleys and hotel rooms disappeared beneath the promise of his taking her to bed—her bed. If they made it that far.

She turned and grasped the doorknob to her bedroom. Jack nipped the back of her neck with his teeth. His thick sex pressed against her buttocks. His broad chest brought searing heat to her skin, which prickled in contrast to the brisk air-conditioned breeze pumping from a vent above them.

Bracing herself on the door, she leaned her forehead against the enameled wood, gasping when Jack's hands tore away the towel and ravished her. His touch seemed everywhere at once—caressing, probing, tickling, teasing. The more she moaned, the more he explored, the more she wanted to widen her stance and allow him immediate entrance into her body and soul.

He breathed the words into the back of her neck, reading her thoughts. "Open for me. Trust me."

His kisses slid down her back as he bent to one knee, his hands encircling her ankles and guiding her legs apart. His humid breath tickled the curls between her thighs, and she pooled again with a slick natural lotion.

"I can't," she protested, her heart banging against her ribs, her breath panting and quick.

He suckled the back of her knee. "You taste like candy."

His mouth rose to the inside of her thigh. "You smell like hot oil."

Fingers plunged into her. She sucked in her breath so hard, her lungs ached. She closed her eyes and bit her lip, fearful she'd draw blood, anticipating the feel of him inside her, here, against the door. She'd treasure every sensation.

"Let me, angel. Please."

He stood, grabbed her hips and pulled her so the tip of his arousal pressed against her throbbing flesh. Even so near, he felt a million miles away. Nothing but inside would be close enough. Nothing but now would be fast enough.

"Let me in." He slipped his hand onto her abdomen, rubbing, coaxing lower, parting her moistness for his entrance, driving her past the limits of thought.

"Yes, Jack, yes."

He needed no more. He entered her swiftly, filling her snugly and fully. The ensuing blast of sensation sent her mind tumbling, and her hand slipped down the door, catching on the knob at the last minute. He rescued her from collapsing by bracing her with his knees, pressing them against hers like a bridge and increasing the support with one arm.

"Damn, I love how tight you are."

His oath preceded his second thrust. When he pushed deeper, she didn't bother to catch the soft scream torn from her throat. Her breath inverted at the same moment he pulled back, and every inch of her responded to the slow, slick slide.

With his mouth, he loved her shoulders and neck. With his hands, he adored her arms, hips, abdomen and breasts. At any moment, she felt sure she'd faint from the explosive sensations rushing through her like a tidal wave.

He pressed into her again, this time delving deeper, groaning from the back of his throat. The ecstasy in the sound injected her with the awareness of her power over him, despite her position. She shifted her weight, found her balance, repositioned her hands on the door and tilted her bottom slightly, knowing when to stop by the trill from his lips.

"Yeah. Oh, yeah. Angela..."

She moved again, concentrating on the thickness inside her, how it left no nerve ending untouched or unattended. In moments, they found a rhythm. She threw her head back, groaning when he laved her neck, gasping when he pinched her nipples, screaming when he fanned his fingers into her pulsing folds and played her till she surrendered to orgasmic release.

She fell forward, her balance steadied by her arms pressed against the door. As her knees buckled, Jack clutched her hips, and she felt him burst with shuddering pleasure.

Once their tremors subsided, Jack withdrew and twirled her around to erase any lingering regrets with his kiss. He hadn't intended to make love to her anywhere but in her bed, so certain was he that she'd balk at this unconventional fantasy. Again, she surprised him with her trust and passion. Last night, she'd nearly convinced him she'd never give him the healing he needed. Now his hopes soared. Lifting her like a feather, he opened the door to the bedroom and pushed them inside.

The bed was all Angela—a four-poster with a thick floral comforter and six fluffy shams atop the queen-size mattress. Sunlight streaked through the drawn, slatted shades, beaming golden shafts where he set her down. He intended to love every inch of skin touched by every ray of light.

Her skin was flushed from their lovemaking, her eyes half-closed but dark with desire. This time he'd make love to her more sweetly.

Then a door slammed.
Angela bolted upright.
A young voice echoed from the hall.
"Mom?"

9

"Mom?" Jack echoed, disbelieving what he'd so clearly heard.

Angela scrambled off the bed, her face pale. She snatched the towel and, after kicking his discarded clothes and the manila envelope inside the bedroom, grabbed the doorknob and yanked.

She covered the slam of the bedroom door by saying, "Dani, honey, is that you?"

Dani?

Angela was a mom?

For a minute, he couldn't breathe. A daughter? A son? A child? A thousand questions crashed through his brain with the force of a runaway truck. He utilized all his recovery power to throw on his pants and shirt.

As he pushed his shirttails into his waistband, he leaned against the closed door, trying not to think about what just happened against that door, hoping to decipher the muffled conversation on the other side.

But Angela undoubtedly hustled the youngster farther into the house, away from him. He was a secret. Just like the child. His honest angel had developed a real knack for lying. Okay, not lying exactly, but omitting the truth. One was just as bad as the other, right?

Either way, Jack's heart plummeted. Angela didn't trust him. As hard as he'd tried to reestablish a bond between them, she still kept secrets. Important ones.

Imaginative lovemaking and a successful business relationship hadn't allowed him entrance into the most intimate portion of her life.

What should he do now? Try to leave?

No. The kid had come in through the front door. Jack had parked in the driveway. If the child had seen the Mustang, his departure would create tough questions for Angela. Besides, he intended to find some answers himself. His only option was to sit tight and wait for Angela to give him his cue.

He glanced around while he buttoned his shirt. Her bedroom reflected its occupant—pretty, floral, cozy, but not cluttered or cutesy. Dark rosewood furniture contrasted against walls painted a pale sage green. And in the center of the antique dressing table was the standard grammar-school-issue photograph of a blond-haired cherub with missing front teeth.

Dani. Short for Danielle, maybe?

He picked up the manila envelope from the floor and slid it onto the table under a homemade paperweight undoubtedly fashioned by unskilled but well-meaning little hands.

She had a daughter.

Examining the picture on the table, he decided the child looked nothing like Angela. Her features favored the lighter side of the spectrum—light green eyes, pale skin, blond hair. Angela's coloring was bolder, darker. He sat on a corner of the bed clutching the photograph, wondering who had fathered the little angel. Who had had a child with *his* angel?

Confusion rocked him. How could Angela fail to mention she had a child? A child who nearly walked in on their lovemaking. His heart pounded against his chest like a sledgehammer. He'd had many a close call in his time. Never one like this.

Laying the picture facedown on the bed, he cradled his head in his hands. So this was why she'd been reluctant to invite him to her home. Did she think he wouldn't be interested in her if he knew she had a child? Or did she want to keep their relationship basic—sex or business, but nothing personal? Either way, Angela had kept a secret from him—something he'd never thought she'd do. Angela Harris never lied. Never until now.

From the moment they'd reunited, Jack had been desperately trying to convince Angela that he'd changed from the callous boy who treated her badly to a man who wanted to explore a future together. What if Angela, too, had changed, and not just in her attitudes about sex?

The thought hadn't occurred to him before. He'd been a poor judge of character in the past, with Lily as his prime example. Still, he wouldn't make up his mind until he'd spoken with Angela. Good liars are born, not made, and Angela could never pull off even the simplest practical joke.

But if this was a joke on him, he certainly wasn't laughing.

"HONEY, I DIDN'T KNOW you were coming home with Aunt Kelly." After tucking the towel securely around her, Angela led her child from the hall and plied her with several enthusiastic hugs. Close call or not, Angela hadn't seen Dani in a week. If the child felt her heart thudding against her ribs, she gave no indication. In the living room, Angela sat on the couch and opened her arms for another embrace. She breathed in the scent of

Dani's hair and marveled in the feel of her arms around her neck.

"The creek at the camp was gonna flood." The nine-year-old stepped away and pushed back her baseball cap. "The counselors were going to call you. Aunt Kelly said I should just come home with them and surprise you."

"And what a great surprise, sweetie." She pecked Dani lightly on the cheek and hugged her again.

I'm going to kill you, Kelly.

"Gosh, Mom. I've only been gone a week."

A knock sounded on the front door before it eased open. "Knock, knock!" Angela pulled Dani in front of her, mindful of her undressed state, then relaxed when only her sister's dark head poked around the door.

"Angela? Whose car is that? And why are you in a towel?"

Angela looked down and caught Dani's equally inquisitive green-eyed stare.

"I was just about to take a shower for a dinner meeting. In fact, I better scoot before my associate comes out of my office and sees me in a towel."

Dani started excitedly down the hall. "Is it Nan? I made her something—"

Angela's towel loosened when she reached to grasp Dani's shoulder. With little grace, she managed to capture both.

"It's not Nan. It's someone you haven't met, and they're using the phone. Listen, Kelly, can Dani go over to your place and play until I've showered and dressed? I'll come right over."

She thanked heaven her sister lived next door.

"We were going to have pizza," the child whined,

digging her hands into the pockets of her jeans. "And Mom, you always take forever to get ready."

Angela inhaled deeply and threw a sharp look at Kelly.

Her sister took the hint. "Come on, Dani. We'll go unpack the van and let her take her shower. Then we'll go for pizza. That way, your mom and her friend can come along."

"Can we go to the mall after?"

Angela gazed briefly heavenward. Only her daughter would practice expert negotiation at a time like this. "If we finish dinner early, yes. If not, I'll take you tomorrow night, I promise. Now, scram."

Bending down, Angela accepted another kiss from her daughter, then gave her a good-natured push toward the door. Kelly went, as well, but stopped when Dani was out of earshot.

Her smile was mischievous. "Anyone I know?"

Angela hated when Kelly acted so big-sisterly smug.

"Yes, as a matter of fact." Angela leaned on the front door and forced her sister out. Just before she slammed it tight, she whispered, "Jack Sullivan."

On her journey down the hall, delight at Kelly's wide-eyed gasp deserted her. She could almost hear the famous line from her favorite late-night rerun. "Lucy, you got some 'splainin' to do."

Clutching her towel, she pushed the door open. She leaned on the threshold until Jack looked up from where he lay on the bed, his arm draped across his forehead.

"I guess we need to have that talk now," she said.

"Is Dani short for Danielle?"

"Danae. It's Greek."

He nodded. "She doesn't look anything like you."

Angela shrugged. "She's adopted."

Silence.

"Look, my sister took her next door to her house, but I promised we'd go out for pizza. You don't have to go, but you're more than welcome."

Jack nodded again.

"I'm going to shower. I'll be quick. Make yourself at home. There's soda in the fridge. And aspirin in the cabinet."

He leaned on his elbows. "Sure you want me poking around? You might have some other secrets...like a husband in the closet."

Angela crossed to the master bath. "No. Just one daughter."

She'd twisted the faucet to hot when Jack knocked. Despite the intimacies they'd shared, she instinctively tightened her grip on her towel and opened the door.

"I just wanted to say I'm sorry." His gaze was off-center and his voice contrite.

"For what?" As far as she could tell, she was the one who should apologize. She'd kept the secret.

He ran his hand through his hair, tugging so hard she could see the tension in his scalp. "For what your daughter almost saw. I didn't know."

Her throat constricted as if she'd swallowed a hot coal. She took two steps to the threshold, then reached up and smoothed the lines from his face. "You had no way of knowing."

He nodded and turned, exiting with the tired gait of someone who'd revisited a painful past. She admired him for his reaction, remembering how his mother had brought lovers home like groceries. Jack truly didn't want to become like his parents. She should have known.

As promised, Angela showered hastily, dabbing on a touch of makeup and twisting her hair in a clip before throwing on jeans, a Broadway T-shirt and tennis shoes. She didn't keep Jack waiting any longer than she had to. His imagination could lead him closer to the truth than she wanted.

She found him sitting in the family room, a photo album spread across his lap. Peeking over his shoulder, she recognized the album as the one containing all her vacation pictures since Dani's birth nine years ago. Chryssie loved to travel, and having a baby hardly slowed her down. When she could get away from college and work, Angela tagged along. After Chryssie's death, Angela kept the tradition alive by planning excursions for Dani whenever time allowed.

"That's Napa." She slid onto the couch and scooted over so half the album fell across her left thigh. "Four years ago, I think."

"After Chryssie died," he surmised.

"Just after. The next year, in fact. She died there, or did I tell you?"

"A car accident?"

"Yeah." She sat back and took a deep breath while Jack flipped the page. With so few people genuinely interested in Chryssie's life or death, she hadn't told the story often. Each time she did, she opened the wound. "She'd hooked up with a dashing French winemaker she'd met in Versailles. He took her to Napa to check out the American competition. It was raining. He wasn't familiar with the road."

She stopped, still finding it difficult to recount the tragedy without a slight rasp in her voice.

"Dani looks a lot like her." He traced his finger lazily over a close-up of the child. "She's beautiful."

Half of her inflated with motherly pride. The other felt a dulled but effective stab of jealousy.

"She's Chryssie's daughter. I adopted Dani after Chryssie died."

The hurt in his eyes made her flinch.

"Why didn't you tell me? It's not like you were married, not that a divorce would have made a difference to me. Why didn't you just tell me about Dani from the start?"

He closed the book and slid it onto its usual spot on the coffee table.

"I didn't want to complicate things," she said, thankful the words came in such a clever disguise. No matter the lie they shielded, the sentiment remained true. Chryssie's letter, received at the reading of the will, made her preference quite clear. She didn't want Angela searching for Dani's birth father. Ignoring her request was the most complex thing Angela had ever done. "I didn't expect we'd see one another after the reunion. I didn't feel it necessary to tell you something so intimate."

"What about later?" He sat forward, balancing his elbows on his lap. "When you knew differently?"

She grabbed a throw pillow and hugged it to her chest. "I didn't want to get involved, remember? That was your idea."

He chuckled sardonically. "Just mine, huh? Get off it, angel. You knew as well as I did that we'd be spending more than just one night together—and that our relationship would be more than business as usual. You should have told me once you asked for my help with your project."

No matter her intentions or long-range concerns, Jack

was right. Maybe he would have turned tail then, sparing her this torturous explanation.

"I didn't know you hated kids, Jack, or I would've told you right from the start." She stood, flung the pillow into the nearby lounge chair and stalked to the kitchen for a soda.

"Hate kids?" He followed, nearly knocking into her when she backed up to close the refrigerator door. "I love kids. More than you know. More than you'd believe. That isn't the point. What I hate are secrets. I hate what you assume about me."

"You have no idea what I think." She couldn't manage the strength to pop open the top of the soda can. She leaned against the counter, drawing her hand to her forehead in a vain attempt to diffuse a headache.

He crossed in front of her, bracing his hands on the counter on either side of her, speaking to the top of her head.

"I know exactly what you think, because for a long time, you were right. Who would want a long-term relationship with Jack Sullivan, son of a deadbeat, lost-in-the-beatnik-era father and a mother who changes husbands with every new moon? He's afraid of commitment, he's convinced he'll end up with ten different kids by four different mothers and no family to speak of, just like dear old Dad."

She didn't bother protesting. He was dead-on.

"That's who I might have become. Lord knows I was on that road. But I don't want children who don't know their father."

Children who don't know their father. His words were like a wrench, twisting her heart and lungs. She hugged herself tighter. *Damn you, Chryssie. Damn you and your secrets.*

"That's when I came home," he whispered, his breath tickling her forehead. "That's when I looked for you."

She glanced up sheepishly. "I thought *I* looked for *you.*"

His tentative smile disarmed her defensive stance. "I'd hoped we'd looked for each other. I'd hoped we could find the new people we'd become, holding on only to the good parts from the past."

Like Dani. Only she wasn't from Jack and Angela's past, but Jack and Chryssie's. "I don't know if there's anything in our past worth holding on to," she admitted, suddenly claustrophobic as his cologne assaulted her with its enticing aroma. Was it her imagination, or did the scent of their lovemaking mingle with the ocean-fresh smell?

He took a step back, though he kept his hands glued to the counter, trapping her, blocking any escape.

"You don't mean that. I don't know what you're afraid of, angel. At least, I don't know yet. But it must be something big for you to lie to me. Whatever you fear, we can work it out."

"What if we can't, Jack?" She realized more clearly how serious Jack was about exploring their relationship. He had no idea of the consequences on her, on him. On Dani.

He slid his palm onto the small of her back. "I've never known you to be such a fatalist. So you have a daughter. Okay, now the game changes, but the payoff increases. I like kids, Angela. I just wasn't prepared for you to have one."

She took the opportunity to break away from him. "And now Dani's home. I have to think about her. You saw what almost happened today. And you obviously remembered what it felt like as a child to have a parent bring lovers home."

The stricken look on his face, a brief shadow that passed over his features like a wraith, told her she'd hit a sensitive mark.

"I can't involve myself with just anyone," she continued. "She's a part of me, so she's a part of my relationships."

From the way his eyebrows pinched together, she knew she'd hurt him again. "I'm not just anyone, angel."

"I know. I didn't mean..."

She didn't know what she meant. Yes, she did. She just couldn't tell him. If he'd reacted so strongly to the fact she'd kept Dani a secret, how would he feel learning the child might be his daughter? He said he liked kids, but he could reevaluate his assessment once he learned of the deception Chryssie had started and Angela had continued without any consideration for his feelings. And if he did like kids and wanted one of his own, he could sue for custody.

She couldn't take that chance.

"Knock, knock." Kelly's voice sounded from the foyer.

Angela had to start locking her doors.

"We're in the kitchen." Angela put the unopened soda in the refrigerator and braced herself on the handle.

Kelly had never liked Jack. She'd spent the majority of Angela's senior year criticizing him. She'd practically burned him in effigy after they'd broken up.

"Jack Sullivan." Kelly entered the kitchen with her arms crossed. "Just as handsome as ever. It's great to see you."

Kelly moved to hug him, and Jack responded in kind. Angela gripped the door handle tighter to keep from falling over.

"The years have been as good to you as they've been to your sister." They broke the friendly embrace. "I hear you and Garrett have two boys. I'm looking forward to meeting them."

"Family life is a great life," Kelly said with a dramatic sigh. "I highly recommend it."

At this, Angela couldn't help but staring, wide-eyed and openmouthed, at her sister.

Hello? Earth to Kelly? Okay, who are you and what have you done with my real sister?

"I'll keep your testimonial in mind." Jack glanced at Angela just in time to catch her snapping her mouth closed.

"Listen, we can catch up at the Pizza Palace. The kids are going to eat the remote control and possibly the TV, too, if we don't leave soon. You are coming, Jack? I mean, you seem to know a little about my life, and I don't know a thing about yours. I didn't even know you were back in town."

Jack dug his hands into his pockets. Angela gulped, recognizing the gesture as one of Dani's standard moves when she felt slightly uncomfortable.

Coincidence. Gestures weren't genetic. Were they?

"I've learned recently that your sister is one of the finest secret keepers in the Western Hemisphere."

Angela shook her head, disbelieving. Maybe she should have confided in Kelly about Jack and Chryssie before now. Maybe she should have warned her he was in town and on the prowl. Maybe the powers that be should develop an anti-Jack charm vaccine for all females within a two-hundred-mile radius.

Whatever the case, she'd lost a potential ally in her personal war to keep Jack out of her life. Of course, Kelly didn't know the whole story. A few long overdue confessions, and she could defect.

"Yes, well." Angela reluctantly snatched her purse. "Let's not keep the troops waiting. One well-known secret is how ornery those three hooligans become when they're hungry."

After Angela pushed brusquely by them, Kelly accepted Jack's proffered arm. Angela suddenly craved pizza. She longed for something spicy in her system. The sugary sweetness in her kitchen nearly made her ill.

HER SISTER kept up the glittery small talk until Garrett and Jack took the kids to the arcade area of the family restaurant after they'd demolished two extra-large pizzas and four hot fudge sundaes. The minute the kids disappeared behind a mirrored wall with the men trailing behind, the plastered smile dropped from Kelly's face. She grabbed Angela's hand, nearly knocking her last slice of pepperoni into Dani's half-melted ice cream.

"Are you nuts?" Kelly asked, her voice only barely in check. "What are you doing messing around with that man again? Didn't you learn your lesson ten years ago?"

"Messing around? Nuts? Excuse me, but you've been treating the guy like he's a Greek god in need of constant adoration since you saw him in the kitchen. Now you're laying into me for making a brilliant business deal with him. I hate to break it to you, sis, but I'm not the one who's playing Sybil."

Kelly scooted forward in the booth, snatching Angela's third slice of pizza and slapping it onto a plate before she managed a bite. "I'm not kidding, Ange. When you had him at your house, and you in only a towel, I didn't know what to think. I decided to play nice in case you'd, I don't know, fallen in love with him again. Now I know it's just a business arrangement, I can try to knock some sense into you. Before it's too late."

Angela pushed the pizza away and opted for a napkin and a slushy diet soda. "It's already too late."

Kelly's face grew ashen. "You didn't?"

Angela poked her straw absentmindedly into her ice.

"Angela?"

When a man at the booth behind them peeked over his shoulder and grinned, her sister moved closer.

"Even after ten years, I still can't erase him from my mind. I've never been able to, especially after..."

"Especially after what?"

The time had come. Angela wasn't sure if she could manage the truth after all this time, but she didn't have a choice. She didn't want to cope with this alone.

"Especially after I realized that in all likelihood, Jack is Dani's biological father."

Slowly, Kelly slid into her seat, sat openmouthed for a minute, then moved back.

"When?"

The vague, single-word question spoke volumes. Angela took a deep breath. Her sister wouldn't be pleased at the amount of time that had passed since she'd first suspected.

"About three months after I visited Richard Lassiter."

Her mouth dropped open again. "That was over a year ago! Why didn't you tell me?"

Angela shook her head. "I didn't see any reason to upset you if I didn't have to."

"I don't understand." Kelly recovered her self-assurance. "Did Richard Lassiter just tell you he wasn't Dani's father? I mean, you told me the trip went well. He and Chryssie were together all the time until graduation."

"Obviously, not *all* the time," Angela quipped.

"But how do you know?"

"I don't. Not for sure. Jack doesn't have any idea I suspect. I've been very careful to keep Dani away from him, until your little surprise this afternoon."

"Ange, I didn't..."

She placed her hand comfortingly on her older sister's. "I know. Anyway, when I visited Richard, I also met his wife, who'd heard by way of the grapevine that I'd adopted. Seems they'd been trying to adopt since they married and they wondered how I'd managed since I was single."

"Richard didn't know about Dani?"

"Very few people in our graduating class really knew Chryssie. Those who did only knew her through me. I guess the gossip mill never caught wind of Dani's parentage. Janie, Richard's wife, was really emotional about the adoption thing. We were having drinks before dinner when she told me Richard was sterile—always had been. He made a joke about wasting money on condoms when he was in school."

Kelly took a large swallow of her drink, tossing it back like whiskey rather than orangeade.

"So Richard can't be Dani's father."

"Nope," Angela confirmed.

"But Jack was your boyfriend. If memory serves me, he and Chryssie didn't even like each other."

"Apparently, they liked each other more than anyone thought." At least with her sister, she didn't have to hide the bitterness. "I didn't suspect Jack until I dug up some old diaries. But even they were vague. I won't know anything concrete until I come straight out and ask him about Chryssie—and I'm not sure I'm going to do that yet."

"There's no one else?" Kelly's face was slightly hopeful.

"For goodness' sake, look at her. Look at him. The shape of their chins. Their eyes. Now that I've seen them together, the resemblance is startling."

Angela caught a glimpse in the wall-length mirrors of the kids, Garrett and Jack. Dani sat in front of Jack on a motorcycle game ride, her feet dangling well above the footrests while Jack held her protectively by the waist. When the machine tilted in a simulated turn, Dani squealed in delight.

Like mother, like daughter.

Not surprisingly, Jack and Dani had hit it off after only five minutes of requisite shyness. Between Jack's consummate charm and Dani's sociable nature, Angela didn't stand a chance at keeping them from bonding.

"What am I going to do?" Angela ran her hands through her hair, then leaned on her elbows to cradle her pounding head.

When her sister remained quiet, Angela looked up. "Kelly?"

"Quiet. I'm thinking."

"Should I be afraid?"

Kelly chastised her with a glare.

"Sorry. I hope you're thinking about what I should do."

Nodding assent, Kelly rubbed the back of her neck, a sure sign her advice might hurt.

"You have to tell him, Angela."

"What? I can't. If he and Chryssie were together, they

only had a one-night stand. They weren't in love. They didn't have a relationship," Angela insisted.

"The brevity of their affair doesn't matter, and you know it. If he's Dani's father, he deserves to know. A parent should never be separated from his child. Chryssie took Dani everywhere with her until she died."

"She didn't want the identity of Dani's father revealed. She stipulated that in the letter I received from the lawyer."

"A letter isn't legally binding. You checked before you went looking for Richard." The detail obviously sparked Kelly's memory. "You were ready to tell him he was the father. Why not Jack?"

Angela winced at a sharp pain at the base of her skull. "Despite their constant fights, Richard and Chryssie loved each other, as much as kids their age could. Richard would have loved Dani for no other reason than because she came from Chryssie."

Kelly glanced into the mirror again. "Looks like Jack's smitten with Dani already. Or is his affection because of you? You know, love the mother, love the child?"

Angela shook her head emphatically. "Jack and I aren't in love. We're just involved in a dangerous case of lust."

Kelly's searching stare expressed her doubt. "And Dani?"

"She's a lovable kid. Who wouldn't want to give her the world after only knowing her an hour?"

Patting Angela's hand, Kelly turned practical. "As long as there's a chance he's the father, he needs to know. It's only right."

"But what if—" She had trouble saying the next few words aloud. "What if he is her father and he wants custody? I could lose her, Kelly. It was hard enough losing Chryssie. I can't take the chance with Dani."

"Do you think he'd do that?" Kelly didn't have a high opinion of Jack, but the surprise in her voice revealed her long-held belief in the inherent goodness of parents everywhere. She'd practically been a parent since age sixteen. Kelly fully understood the statement, "For the good of the child." Unfortunately, not everyone else did.

Angela sat back, closing off her view of Jack and Dani as they slipped more quarters into the motorcycle machine.

"I've lied to him. I've kept a very important secret from him. He has every right to be furious."

"I can buy that. But would he take his anger out on Dani?"

They'd been together for only a few days, and Jack had effectively mangled every preconceived notion she held about him. No longer could she deceive herself with the idea he was a fly-by-night gigolo with only sex as his objective. He'd settled down, and from what she'd seen, he was looking for a woman to settle with.

Yet he'd said he hated secrets. She sensed his loathing of lies came from a deeply painful source.

But could that source have been worse than hers?

"I just don't know, Kelly. I just don't know."

10

"YOU DIDN'T have to carry her," Angela whispered, touched by the way Jack cradled a sleeping Dani in his arms while she unlocked the front door. "She's not so light anymore."

"She's a feather," Jack whispered back. "Besides, this gives me an excuse to come inside."

Angela nodded, entered and disengaged the security alarm while Jack moved inside and quietly pushed the front door closed with his foot. She knew he wouldn't wait until tomorrow to finish the conversation they'd abandoned earlier. After having a ball entertaining Dani at the arcade, then at the mall, he was probably even more convinced a relationship between him and Angela deserved a chance. And if she could manage to forget the secret between them, she might have agreed.

But she couldn't forget. Not for an instant. Not when his face was pressed so close to Dani's that the resemblance was undeniable. Not with Jack's aversion to secrets and lying so perfectly clear.

Angela opened the door to Dani's bedroom and silently slid her still-packed suitcase onto the floor. Jack lay Dani on top of her Looney Tunes comforter, then slipped out of the room while Angela undressed her and tucked her under the covers.

"Mom?" Dani asked sleepily as Angela stepped away from the bed.

"Yeah, honey. What is it?"

"Is Jack still here?" She punctuated the sentence with a yawn.

"Yes, he is. Why?"

"Good." Dani rolled toward Angela and slipped one arm under her pillow and the other around her stuffed Pepe le Pew. "He's a major hunk."

"Excuse me?" Angela asked, smiling.

Dani drifted back to sleep, and Angela wasn't about to wake her to discuss the matter. The topic needed no discussion. Dani hit the nail on the head.

She found her major hunk in the kitchen. Leaning across the breakfast bar from the living room side, she watched him hunt through her cupboards.

"I thought I'd make coffee." He randomly opened cabinets in search of the brew.

She motioned to the fridge. "Coffee's in the freezer. I try not to drink it every day. Too much makes me nervous."

He stopped his search and joined her at the bar. "Then I guess you don't need coffee right now." He reached across the tiled counter and took her hands in his.

When he started rubbing her knuckles with the pads of his thumbs, she tried to focus on her thoughts. Less than a semblance of a touch from him started her veins surging.

"Jack, I have to apologize for not telling you about Dani. I didn't think we'd be together this long. But when I knew, I should have told you."

He nodded, extending his simple ministrations to the sensitive skin of her wrists. "I guess once you start keeping a secret, it's hard to stop."

She took a deep swallow, unable to pull her gaze

away. The man had an uncanny ability to get right to the heart of the matter.

"You have no idea." She retreated to the darkened living room and clicked on a small crystal lamp. The light cast a feeble amber glow. The effect was intimate, romantic. The last thing she needed.

When she grabbed the tassel to click on the overhead ceiling fan light, Jack stopped her.

"There's no need to shed a lot of light tonight. If you have more secrets, they can wait until tomorrow."

He wrapped his hands around her waist and pulled her beside him on the couch.

"We've both had a long day." He sighed and wrapped a protective arm around her, encouraging her to snuggle. "Why don't we just sit here for a few minutes."

She accepted his invitation, marveling at the powerful warmth of his arms and his chest. She closed her eyes, trying to focus solely on the comfort of his embrace. Within seconds, the scent of his cologne, the tautness of his muscles and the smooth strokes of his hand up and down her arm awakened her. Under his command, the most innocent gesture became a fiery seduction.

"You don't really think we can just sit here, do you?" she asked wryly, looking at him.

His gulf-green gaze betrayed a hint of mischief. "Why not? We're adults. We don't have to constantly touch each other."

"We are touching each other." She burrowed deeper against his chest. She shouldn't, but some treats were too delicious to resist. After his reaction this afternoon, she trusted he wouldn't initiate sex. He didn't know that Dani was dead tired, and even when she wasn't, she slept like a rock.

"That's not what I meant," he said with a slight groan. "I mean, touching touching."

"Like this afternoon? Like the other night at your studio? Like the first night we'd seen each other after ten years?"

Jack shifted uncomfortably, careful not to push Angela away in the process. Each question acted as a clear reminder that they couldn't keep their hands off each other. She'd probably meant to get him so frustrated he'd leave, but the memories only reminded him of how pliant, how willing, how sexy she could be.

She moved, as if equally restless. He held her tightly. Maybe she, too, remembered how great they were together. How their bodies fit. How their mouths danced. He groaned.

"Point taken," he conceded, "but I'm not ready to leave."

He turned and pulled her across his lap. Big mistake. Her thighs slid over his. Her hip rested against his groin. Keeping his hands to himself wouldn't be as effortless as he thought.

"Your holding me like this isn't going to make conversation any easier." Her sweet breath caught him just under the chin.

"I wasn't trying to make anything easy," he answered, "I just wanted to look into your eyes."

At his words, she looked away, glancing around the room and down the darkened hall leading to Dani's room.

"She's exhausted. She won't wake up," he reassured her.

"She already woke up once."

"She did? Did she say anything about me?" The question popped out before he could stop it. Entertaining Dani had been a new and satisfying experience, but knowing whether or not she enjoyed herself remained far more important. The feeling pleasantly surprised him.

Angela smiled, apparently touched by his paranoia.

"Actually, she did. She says you're a major hunk."

Jack tried to make his grin look humble, though his chest swelled like the plumage of a peacock. From what little he knew of nine-year-olds, that was high praise. He'd known the munchkin for a little over four hours, but for some reason he didn't quite grasp yet, the child's approval was crucial. He wondered how much of his response had to do with his feelings for Angela and his fiasco with Lily.

"She has a great eye." He hoped conceit would cover his genuine pride.

"I'll have to warn her about men like you. Good-looking and only one thing on their minds." She punched him lightly on the shoulder.

"Right now, I have a hell of a lot of things on my mind."

"And sex isn't one of them?"

"I didn't say that."

"You know—" she squirmed as if she might move off his lap "—I feel like a teenager again, making out after Kelly went to bed."

He leaned his head against the wall. "I remember your sister catching us more than once. If your mother'd been home, you might still be grounded."

"Kelly was a tough cookie, but life wasn't a picnic for her." Angela's gaze drifted to a family photo on the coffee table. Her eyebrows furrowed, and a tiny frown bowed her lips. "She practically raised me, my parents were away so much. Then after Dad died, Mom hardly came home from overseas at all."

Jack nodded in silent agreement, though he really didn't share the same experience. He and his brothers and sisters were scattered across the country.

"I distinctly remember Kelly never liking me. I wonder why she was so nice today."

"She thought we were lovers."

"Aren't we?" He slid her closer until their noses touched.

In the depths of her hazel irises, he caught sight of the maelstrom of confusion rocking her mind—a storm battering him, as well. Since this afternoon, he and Angela could no longer pretend to be unattached players of a sexual game. Though he'd never planned to let her go, she'd expected their relationship to be short-lived. If she intended to break things off now, he needed to understand her motives. Was she just a mother protecting her child, or did she really want a disposable affair?

He'd have to ask. "You're not thinking about breaking things off, are you?"

"Now that Dani's in the picture, I don't know. We saw what almost happened this afternoon."

He agreed and showed her by nodding, allowing the tip of his nose to caress hers. The comfort of the small intimacy abated the resentment toward his mother's indiscreet behavior. How many miserable breakfasts had he endured with a strange man sitting at the other end of the table? Even when his mother's lovers didn't stay all night, did she really think he, no matter how young, was that blind?

When Angela placed a weightless kiss on the corner of his mouth, the memory waned.

Dipping his head, he captured her slightly parted lips, slipping his tongue inside before she could pull away or protest. She did neither. She melted into the cradle of his arms and slipped her hands around his neck.

"Angel, I still want you. Need you. Crave you."

Her soft coo urged him to deepen the kiss, to further explore the recesses of her mouth. Nothing could happen tonight, and nothing would. Yet instead of sexual pursuits, they could find something even more precious.

"Jack." She gasped as she pulled back. "We can't."

"What? We're just kissing. Relax."

How could she say no? Even at this brief parting, she missed the taste, scent and feel of him. Yet how could she relax in his embrace when she harbored such a devastating secret?

"Usually, I can." She glanced away as she sought to form an honest defense. "But I'm really distracted. And tired. I didn't sleep much last night, and knowing Dani, her camp schedule will have her popping out of bed and demanding pancakes at dawn."

He released his hold, allowing her to place her feet on the carpet.

"I make great pancakes," he suggested, though even in the dim light she caught the teasing glitter in his eyes.

She stood, then turned and held out a hand to help him up. "I'm sure you do. Maybe you can come by Sunday morning and whip up a whole stack."

Taking her hand, he started to stand, resignation chiseled into his square jawline. At the last second, he shifted his weight and pulled her into his lap, swallowing her cry of surprise with a kiss.

"I'm there," he murmured, trailing a final path of cottony kisses over her cheeks, chin and eyelids.

She languished in every touch, nearly giddy in the innocent sensuality.

I'm there? "You're where?" she wondered aloud.

He stood, taking her with him in his arms and then placing her firmly on the floor. He obviously tried not to laugh at her disoriented query—but he didn't try hard enough. The corners of his mouth tilted distinctly upward. He covered his merriment with a cough.

"Pancakes, Sunday morning." He pecked her one last time on the cheek before heading toward the door. "Though we can talk about the menu tomorrow."

He let himself out in such a quiet rush, she barely heard the door close. She sat on the couch in the warm indentation he'd left. The man was amazing—patient, generous, trusting to the point of naiveté. But only with her. His cynicism ran deep, dispersing only when it focused on her.

And he was sexy. Devastating. This afternoon, she'd willingly yielded to a fantasy she'd never allowed herself more than a minute to entertain. The results had been explosive, engulfing, mind-shattering. Just remembering made her body tingle with renewed sexual friction.

As the silence settled in, the beating of her heart receded and her schedule for tomorrow scrolled in her brain like the screen on her computer calendar.

Friday. Dani to Kelly's for the day. Ten o'clock meeting with modeling agent. *And Jack.* At noon, they'd meet with her creative team. At three, they'd assemble her marketing crew to finalize the budget. In less than twelve hours, she and Jack would be together again, though this time in a professional capacity.

Before leaving for her Napa Valley vacation, she had to finalize all plans for the Whispering Palms campaign and supervise the shoot. They'd be busy. She wouldn't have a free moment to tell Jack about Dani or to explain Chryssie's reasons for keeping the information to herself. They'd be swamped with scheduling, contracts and brainstorming powwows. She probably wouldn't even have time to spend alone with Jack.

Yeah, right.

She removed her hair clip, shook her head and ran her fingers through her hair. Locking the front door and setting the alarm, she acknowledged that no matter what capacity Jack was in or how overwhelmed with business she was, he possessed a potent magic over her. A magic she couldn't help submitting to.

After turning off the lights, turning down the air conditioner and peeking in one last time at Dani, she went into her room and shrugged out of her jeans and bra, leaving only her T-shirt and panties as pajamas. Once she'd washed off her makeup and brushed her hair, she climbed under her comforter. She turned to click off the lamp when she noticed the envelope under the paperweight.

Hesitantly, she got up and tapped the circular object Dani made at last year's camp. Did she dare look?

Unable to resist, she scurried to lock her door then grabbed her envelope. The chill of the air conditioner and the prospect of seeing Jack's pictures of her resulted in a spread of dimply gooseflesh.

She reclined on the bed, pulled her comforter around her and carefully bent back the metal clasps. Biting her lip, she slid her fingers inside. She stopped at the feel of glossy photo paper. Did she really want to see this? Did she really want to relive her hour as Jack's wanton biker chick?

Of course, she did.

She breathed out an appreciative whistle. "Oh, my."

The man must be a whiz with an airbrush. Of course, she knew Jack wouldn't have retouched the eight-by-tens. Neither beauty nor physical excellence dominated the photos. Self-critical or not, she considered her attractiveness and toned body as typical of many women her age. Yet the pictures shocked her. Her perceptions of herself differed from the image on film. The completely unhindered sexual prowess in her stance, clothes and eyes startled her.

She flipped to the next photo, then the next, hoping to find one that portrayed the Angela she recognized, the woman who sat cuddled on her queen-size bed with no makeup on, her hair disheveled and her body covered by an oversize T-shirt. After examining a dozen shots, she ceased her futile search. Mounted on the bike, her legs stretched out and her breasts straining against the glove-tight leather, her likeness conjured the words Jack had spoken before their first meeting with Davenport.

You are that woman on the Harley.

Could he be right? If he was, he was responsible.

As the photos progressed from merely sexy to blatantly erotic, she lay against the pillows, startled when the scent of Jack's cologne surrounded her with its fresh, breezy scent. He'd reclined there earlier and left his mark.

In the next photo, a close-up, she was ripping the material above her heart, her face enraptured as if Jack sliced open her soul. The glossies revealed pose after pose of raw ecstasy and insatiable need.

She kicked the comforter off her legs.

When she caught sight of her breasts, full and round and heavy, pouring out of her slashed top, a twinge of excitement quickened her breath and dried her mouth. The memory of the passion that had followed, the feel of Jack's mouth thirstily sucking her nipples, his hard sex pressing against her throbbing mons inspired the reaction anew.

The next photo, taken with a telephoto lens from the camera Jack had set on the tripod, mirrored her memory with bold accuracy. Her thighs, alternately visible through the shadowy black lace and uneven tears, flexed as they curved around his waist. His hands, hooked beneath the ruined leather, yanked the material away.

Warmth pooled between her thighs as the images progressed, each more lusty, more hungry, more true to the burning fire that nearly drove them both insane.

Examining one picture closely, she saw his teeth tugging at her nipple and the rapturous expression on her face. Involuntarily, her breasts responded as they had that night—as they had that afternoon. The throb of her need intensified. Her lips desired moisture, but passing her tongue over them only dried them more, multiplying her compulsion to call Jack, to have him return and soothe her ache.

She'd settle for a shower instead. She tucked the sealed envelope beneath her mattress for safekeeping, then threw off her T-shirt and turned on the faucet. She should run the water slightly chilled, though she preferred her shower hot—steamy hot—hot enough to burn Jack's touch right off her skin.

After she'd nearly scalded herself, she turned up the cold water and found a happy medium between blistering and frigid. She turned her back to the showerhead, allowing the massaging water to pelt her neck and shoulders. Resting her head against the tiled wall, she tried not to think anymore. She wanted to relax and let the water assuage her intimate agony.

Facing the water, she stood so the streams rained on her breasts. Instead of cooling the fire Jack had started, the downpour kindled her physical need. She stepped closer, decreasing the distance so the droplets stung her flesh the same way Jack's teeth did when he bit her so seductively.

She turned the heat up and removed the hand-held showerhead. Since Jack couldn't ease her sweet suffering tonight, she'd damn well find some other way.

"NAN, FAX the advertising mock-ups to Davenport right away," Angela instructed. "Then we'll just sit back and wait for his okay. Remember, everyone, budget meeting at three."

Jack snapped the cap on his pen and shoved his hands through his hair. How Angela survived sessions like this one raised his awe of her. Now he knew how she so expertly manipulated his heart into a twisted mass. The woman could manipulate, cajole, inspire and direct the most diverse group of creative personalities into putting together a project that even his inexperienced eyes recognized as impressive.

"Angela, more coffee? Jack?" Nancy offered, scooping the neater set of mock-ups from the conference table as the rest of the creative team shuffled out of the room.

Angela shook her head absently, her gaze locked on the storyboards they'd hashed out for the thirty-second spots. She held Jack's Polaroids, taken during his initial shoot on Wednesday, like a royal flush, and compared them to the drawings in front of her. Her expression, hard and concentrated, revealed nothing, though he did note how she pouted when deep in thought.

She looked beautiful.

Jack, on the other hand, looked like hell. He needed an infusion of something strong enough to erase the painfully structured day from his mind. Not to mention his restless night. Since Angela would never agree to a quickie in her office, coffee would have to do.

"Thanks, Nancy. I'll take a cup."

As an independent photographer, Jack rarely found himself included in such intense meetings. He never planned his private projects, preferring to let them evolve in the field. As for his freelance work, he refused to mix with the corporate types and rarely gave his input ahead of time. His clients would submit preferences before the shoot, and then he'd do whatever he pleased. And they'd be thrilled with the results.

For Angela, he'd made an exception. He'd even taken on the title Director of Photography to make her happy.

She looked at him after dealing the Polaroids onto the boards, setting each one beside the corresponding drawing. A satisfied grin broke halfway through her serious expression.

"This isn't half-bad."

He slid over until he sat beside her. He caught the scent of her perfume, a woodsy scent she probably reserved for work, and wondered how he'd kept himself focused on anything but her all morning. Dressed in a blousy male-style shirt tied casually at the waist of her pleated slacks and covering a skintight tank top underneath, she oozed corporate control and feminine confidence.

"Neither are you."

She smiled, but her lips quivered as if she feared his kiss.

He pushed away from the table, not wanting to make her uncomfortable in her place of business. "I'm impressed. You push your people just enough to get great results. They work hard. They respect you."

"I'm the boss," she said, curling a wayward lock around her ear. "They have to."

He flicked the auburn tress free, then let his finger slide down her cheek. Good intentions. Weak self-control. "You know better than that."

She glanced at him warily, then at the door, twisting her mouth into a reluctant frown. "Jack, we still have work to do. We need to choose which of your photographs will be reproduced as the limited-edition print."

He braided his fingers into her dangling gold chain, tempted to pull her forward and kiss the worried look right off her face. "Not until Davenport calls with his approval for the concept and my fifty percent cut of the profits. Until then, we may have hours to kill."

Less than a day ago, she would have asked him what he had in mind. She would have toyed with him, teased him, enticed him until he had no choice but make love to her on the conference table. But since Dani had returned from camp, he hadn't seen the seductive sprite he'd grown to crave. She wasn't gone, Jack knew. She was simply hidden behind Angela's fear like a mob informant beneath concrete.

But fear of what?

Angela eased the chain from his grasp, pushed her chair back and busied herself with cleaning up the sugar-coated napkins and empty doughnut boxes scattered around the table. "Why don't you see where Nancy is with your coffee?"

Jack accepted her clear dismissal with a chastising cluck of his tongue. "Afraid to be alone with me, angel?"

Was she just tired, or did her face seem to pale when he said the word *alone?*

"Of course not, Jack. Why would I be afraid now?"

He mulled over her words and her jittery expression until Nancy buzzed in on the intercom. "Davenport's on line three."

Angela took a deep breath, swallowed and walked to the phone. Jack backed out of the room, giving her privacy.

He found Nancy by the coffee machine, sent her to her work and poured himself a cup, lightening it with a touch of cream. The break room was small but private, allowing Jack a moment to collect his thoughts while he watched for the red light on line three to go out.

Why was Angela so nervous? With the existence of her daughter revealed, she had no reason to be anxious. Dani was an enchanting child, and he'd fallen instantly under her spell. The fact that she was Chryssie Hart's daughter made no difference to him, except he now thought of his high school nemesis a bit more fondly. She looked hauntingly like Chryssie, but her sparkling personality and bright-eyed honesty were Angela through and through.

So why did he feel as if Angela still harbored some devastating secret?

The instinct to push her gnawed at him, though another part of him wanted to ignore the signals that told him he was in for a shock. He'd convinced himself Angela wasn't like Lily—she didn't keep secrets, she didn't tell lies. Then he'd discovered Dani. What else could there be?

And did the secrets matter?

When line three went dark, he weaved his way back to the conference room. Nancy watched him expectantly the entire way, and the leader of the creative team leaned out of his office. Jack saluted them confidently with his coffee, knocked, then slipped into the room.

He found Angela sitting at the head of the conference table, her eyes staring blankly at the far wall.

"Angela? What's wrong?"

Jack slid into a seat beside her and took her hands in his. Her palms were clammy with cold perspiration.

"Don't tell me he didn't like the presentation. I met the man. He didn't seem stupid to me."

Angela pulled in a shaky breath.

"He's not. He has full confidence this will be the most innovative and effective marketing campaign ever."

Her words should have sounded proud, excited, effervescent.

They didn't.

"Then what's the problem?"

She breathed deeply again, this time pressing her shoulders down and straightening her spine. Turning, she faced him squarely, a no-nonsense tilt to her chin.

"He has high expectations for Harris and Associates. So much so that he made me an unexpected offer."

Jack didn't want to ask. "An offer? Of what?"

For the briefest instant, she glanced down to where Jack's hands locked with hers. If she thought he'd let go, she had another think coming.

"Of a vice-president position in his corporation. He wants to merge Harris and Associates with Davenport

Homes to handle all the marketing for his international development interests."

"But Davenport Homes is located in—"

"California. I know. He wants to see me first thing Monday morning at his San Francisco office."

11

HE WOULDN'T let her go. Okay, so he had no real power over her decision whether or not to move. But he sure as hell didn't plan to roll over and let her relocate without a fight. Not after ten years of missing her. Not after the past week.

Too shocked by Davenport's proposal to discuss it, she'd accepted Jack's offer to make her travel plans while she met with the staff again. She also didn't balk when he made plane reservations for three—Dani and him included.

She'd mentioned an upcoming Napa Valley vacation earlier, so why not combine business with pleasure and invite himself along? If Angela considered, even for a moment, taking this six-figure job, Jack planned to be there to deal dirty.

He would even tell her he loved her.

Except that she wouldn't believe him.

Even if he was close to believing it himself.

During the five-hour plane trip, he entertained Dani, allowing Angela freedom to feign interest in marketing reports and industry journals. Several times, he caught her staring at him and her daughter playing together when she thought he wasn't looking. He sensed her turmoil, felt the strained tension in her grin. Did she wonder what kind of father he'd be? Did this play a part in her decision?

Even if he hadn't fallen in love with Angela, he would have truly adored her child. He found himself so wrapped up in Dani, he hardly noticed the length of the trip, the layover in Dallas, the turbulence over Nevada. By the time they reached the airport and rented a car, Jack knew he wanted to give marriage and fatherhood a try. Lily had denied him that chance. Would Angela?

As they waited to exit the parking lot, Jack glanced at Dani sitting beside him, chattering about Muir Woods, their first destination on their way to Napa. She looked so much like Chryssie. He couldn't help wondering what Angela's children would look like—especially if fathered by him. Would they have his height? His hair? Her large hazel eyes and generous lips?

His stomach roiled, more from expectation than fear. How many hours would pass before he could get Angela alone, even for a minute, to soothe his yearning to touch her? He pulled up to a stop sign, frowning. So far, Angela had managed to use Dani and Davenport's offer as shields to keep him at a safe distance.

Jack pulled into traffic, his determination renewed. By night's end, he'd break through every barrier Angela set around her heart—even if he had to let down his own barriers to do it.

WITH A WEEKEND to enjoy before her Monday meeting with Davenport, Angela strolled Muir Woods, following the peaceful pathways she and Dani enjoyed every year. Jack pulled out his camera, snapping Dani posing next to a redwood, enticing a squirrel, balancing on the fence by the brook. Angela tried not to be jealous of their newfound bond, but it wasn't easy.

She'd never had to share Dani before, at least never with a man. If Jack did turn out to be Dani's biological father, the ramifications would be more gut-wrenching than she'd imagined. Especially if he didn't want the job.

The weekend accommodations Allistair Davenport arranged at a winery impressed her and filled her with dread. The sprawling Victorian-style bed-and-breakfast with guest cottages situated down a private drive from the public wine-tasting and welcome center afforded solitude. Beauty. Romance.

Behind them, grapevines snaked up carefully tended trellises, stopping only when blocked by a limestone hill. An English-style garden wrapped around the house, replete with miniature rose blossoms, fragrant lilac and vivid mums. In such a setting, how could she fight her desire for Jack?

"This is better than the hotel!" Dani exclaimed, skipping down a stone path. "Can I pick flowers for Mom's memorial?"

The words were forthright and innocent, so like Dani, and yet they stung Angela's heart. When had Dani become so used to the idea of her mother being dead? When would *she?*

"We'll ask the manager, sweetie."

Dani continued toward their cottage, allowing privacy enough for Jack to wrap his arm tentatively around her waist, creating a rebellious thrill in her belly. "You're going there tonight?"

Angela indulged herself, shifting her weight so her cheek brushed against his jacket. She'd explained the ritual on the plane, saving him the surprise. "We usually go in the morning, when it's prettiest. I let Dani make the plans, you know?"

He didn't, but he saw the wisdom in allowing Dani to take the lead. Even though he didn't have a particularly good relationship with either of his parents, they were both alive and well. He'd never known his grandparents. Losing someone to death was an event he hadn't experienced. Dani's resilience impressed him. Humbled him.

"Do you think she wants me along?"

A strange emotion flashed across Angela's face, something akin to fear but not fear itself. More like dread, yet more resigned. Inevitable.

"She hasn't said she didn't."

"Should I ask?"

Angela watched her feet as they walked. "I'm sure it'll be all right. As far as she knows, you were Chryssie's friend."

Jack let the topic drop with the same swiftness as his hand from her waist. Hypocrisy wasn't his forte, and now wasn't the time to reopen wounds. Yet he respected Chryssie for never telling Angela about their mistake—for never surrendering to cleansing her guilt at Angela's expense.

Dani led the way to the guest house, a tall-roofed, gingerbread cottage just behind the garden. She flung open the front door, revealing a warm, oak-paneled room decorated in sepia tones of gold and brown, with touches of scarlet in pillows and throw rugs to add vivacity. Two bedrooms, connected by a huge bathroom with a garden tub, lay to the right. A small but cozy eat-in kitchen inhabited the left corner of the house. A circular staircase led to an open loft containing a walnut sleigh bed, a dresser and a closet-size half bath.

Despite the time change and the lengthy flight, Dani still had the energy to bound up the stairs and claim the loft as hers.

"Wouldn't you rather share a bedroom down here

with me?'' Angela asked, ignoring how cowardly the question sounded in Jack's presence.

One exasperated glance from Dani over the railing gave her her answer.

"Nice try." Jack's whisper mocked her as much as his attendant wink.

They settled in quickly, surprised when the public relations manager for the winery appeared with an impressive dinner for three—courtesy of Allistair Davenport. They feasted on roasted venison, fresh garden vegetables, a wine-sauced crème brûlée and a hamburger, crispy fries and a chocolate sundae for Dani. The man knew how to sweeten a deal.

They stacked the dishes together, like a family. Jack needed a lesson or two in the proper way to scrape food from a dish, but otherwise, he slipped into domesticity with an ease that warmed Angela's heart. How could she have been so wrong?

He'd make a great husband and he'd be a good father for Dani. His craving for parenthood shone like a beacon in his eyes, though she wondered if he knew.

He wasn't his father—he was Jack. He'd sworn since the reunion he'd changed, that he wouldn't hurt her. And he hadn't. Not as she would hurt him when he learned the truth.

After Angela sent Dani in for a bath, Jack poured her another glass of dessert wine and pulled her onto the couch beside him. Fingers entwined, they spoke about nothing important, though Jack's touch said volumes.

Her entire body ached to climb into his lap and feel his muscled heat thrust against her. The tilt of his head, the curve of his smile, all told her he wanted to make love with her tonight. And yet, the vibes jetting from his fingertips were sweet and warm and comforting.

Which she found even more sexy.

Dani's eyes were heavy-lidded when she emerged from the bathroom, so Angela tucked her into bed. Jack said good-night from downstairs, then disappeared into his room.

Angela wanted a bath, but didn't dare enter the bathroom as long as Jack's light shone from under the adjoining door. The house was too quiet, the atmosphere too romantic, her libido too aroused, for her to take a chance.

Her mind swirled with regrets over her secret and Davenport's offer. She knew she wouldn't take the job. Increased pay and prestige weren't worth the high price.

From the start, the trip had been a ruse. She couldn't let Davenport think she hadn't considered his generous proposition. She wanted to keep his business. She just didn't want to move away from her family and friends.

Away from Jack.

She would tell him about Dani. He had a right to know of her suspicions, to try to discover if they were true. Every instinct told her she'd been wrong to keep this from him. Now, she had to find the words.

How he reacted would be up to him. His anger would be understandable, justified and unbearable. But if he loved her the way she loved him, he'd find a way to forgive.

The realization of her feelings didn't shock her in the least. Deep in her heart, she knew she'd loved him all along, probably since high school and definitely since the reunion. He'd stuck in her system not because she hadn't slept with him, but because he'd ingrained himself into her soul—the soul he'd wanted her to surrender before she knew how.

She tossed a light sweater over her shoulders and took the last of her wine onto the porch. The night, still and quiet, glittered with the glow of gas lamps in the garden. The heady scent of grapes and jasmine hung heavy in the air, kissing her skin with sweetness and allowing her to relax.

She didn't see Jack on the porch until she heard the familiar click and whir of his camera.

"I love night shots."

His voice was wistful, full of delight and serenity. What would it sound like after he knew what she'd kept from him? A shiver shook her from head to toe.

"Cold?" He removed his camera from around his neck and stepped closer. His body warmth and masculine scent enticed her like a toasty blanket on a winter day.

She backed away until her shoulder met with the rough doorway arch. "It's chilly tonight."

He placed the camera on a chair. "Want me to warm you?"

"I'll be fine." She stared into his green gaze with all the insistence she could muster, though her declaration faltered under the power of his presence. Whenever she managed to forget the secret between them, she could think of nothing but being with him, alone. When their hands had touched on the luggage carousel, she'd drawn back as if burned. When he had brushed an errant curl out of her face at the redwood forest, her skin had tingled with delight.

How long could she last until her body betrayed her? Again.

Amusement lit his eyes like opals. "You're shivering."

"Let's go inside, then."

"Not just yet." He trapped her against the wall, then smoothed his hands over her hips. "Out here, I have a good reason to touch you, to kiss you, to heat you up the way you like." His touch slid over her buttocks. "Tell me you want me. Tell me, and I will."

She closed her eyes and tried to think. Sadness gripped her, forcing her to acknowledge that now was the time to tell him about his possible paternity.

But the admiration in his eyes stopped her. Despite their shared past and romantic liaisons, their relationship was still new and vulnerable. When all was said and done, would they have anything left? They might find themselves pitted against each other for Dani's custody. Nothing could annihilate their desire more quickly.

He placed a light kiss on the corner of her mouth, then explored the length of her arms with his hands. Stealthily, he wedged his knee between her unsteady legs and pressed her against the cold wood.

Only three words came to her mind.

"I want you."

Slipping her arms under his, she pulled herself into his embrace and buried her face in his chest. He crowned her with a light kiss, then smoothed her hair sweetly. Yet the gesture didn't last long. It couldn't. Not for them. Not ever.

He bent, slid his arms beneath her knees and cradled her into his chest.

"I was hoping you'd say that."

Jack carried her inside and set her on the bed.

"Wait here," he said.

Angela kicked off her shoes and removed her sweater. Jack locked the door, lit several candles and took them into the bathroom. She slid onto the bed, letting her weight sink into the goose down comforter.

One more night of secrets wouldn't hurt. One more night of loving might hold her over through the anger, the resentment, the fury he was sure to unleash. Then again, if she imparted the news in the light of morning, with the glow of lovemaking still fresh, maybe he'd be more inclined to understand.

The sound of running water brought her attention to Jack. Golden candlelight outlined his lean frame, inclined confidently against the doorjamb. He'd unbuttoned and untucked his shirt, looking rumpled and sexy and male.

"Have you noticed the fixtures in here?" A note of lusty mischief lilted in his voice.

She slipped off the bed, allowing her gaze to dip below the waistband of his jeans.

"Those aren't the fixtures I'm interested in."

His tilted grin mirrored his pleasure at her tease.

"Oh, but you really should see them."

He moved sideways when she walked by, allowing her to enter in front of him. When she stopped just past the paper-thin freestanding screen, he slid his hands around her waist and buried his lips in her neck.

The fixtures were gold, or at least they appeared to be under the sparkle of the candles Jack had placed around the room. Two bottles of wine chilled in a sinkful of ice, and a Jacuzzi steamed with running hot water.

Slowly, Jack unzipped her dress and drew the straps over her arms until the light cotton material fluffed around her ankles. Covering her neck, shoulders and back with alternately languid and intense kisses, he undid her bra and tossed it aside.

"You are so delicious," he murmured. When gooseflesh prickled her skin, he rubbed her arms rhythmically, stoking her skin like smoldering embers. "I'm going to taste every inch of you, angel. Every inch."

She slipped his shirt off, placing deep kisses on his chest. "Promise?"

"Wait." He punctuated the command with his mouth over hers. His lips, moist and steamy like the air, molded to hers as if created solely for the purpose of kissing her. The joining, brief but powerful, left her dizzy as he stepped to the sink and retrieved a bottle of wine and a corkscrew.

"I think you'd be best with a red wine, don't you?"

She smiled and joined him, unbuckling his belt. He slid the cork from the bottle as his pants dropped to the floor.

"Glasses?" she asked, delighted by the look in his eyes when she slipped out of her panties and tugged down his boxers. She wanted him desperately. And she knew why.

She couldn't say the words aloud, but undeniable love swelled in her heart. He excited her, thrilled her in every fiber of her body and soul.

"No glasses." Jack led her to the tub. She sat on the edge and made a sizzling sound when her bare feet met the heated water.

He stepped around her, easing her legs apart as he knelt. Candlelight, hazy from the rising steam, flickered around him. The emerald depths of his irises caught the flames and reflected them with an intensity that made her hungry for his kiss.

Slipping one hand around her back, he steadied her, then poured, letting the icy wine flow from the top of her shoulder to her breast. She flinched, then gasped when he bent forward and licked the wine away. His warm tongue traced a zigzag path downward, lightly sipping the last drop clinging to her nipple.

"I was right," he said huskily, lifting his head slowly and kissing her from chin to mouth. "You are delicious."

The wine lingering on his lips, robust and fruity, awakened every dormant nerve. Then he took another sip of wine from the bottle but didn't swallow until after he had her other nipple between his lips. The contrasting feel of the hot water, the cold wine and the gentle tug on her breast made her gasp.

Only his hand bracing her thigh kept her seated when he doused her again, this time letting the wine splash down her chest, past her stomach, trickling like tiny drops of ice into her curled mound, touching her intimately. The sensations fired her, and she nearly shook with rapture as he licked the crimson liquid away, inebriating her with his powerful intoxicant.

As he dipped his head to find the last few drops, she ran her fingers through his hair. Spreading her knees wide, she clutched him, vaguely aware he'd set the wine bottle beside her. His hand, chilled from the ice, traced her inner thigh while his tongue found her budded center.

"Oh, Jack, stop, please, stop." She knew his simple ministrations would take her to the edge too soon. She wanted him to go with her, inside her, sharing the explosion of light she could already see just beyond the insides of her eyelids.

With one last lick, he kissed a trail up her neck, easing his hands down her back to cup her buttocks. As he stood her in the rising water of the tub, she took the wine bottle and poured the Cabernet over his shoulders and down his chest.

His eyes flashed wide. The liquid, warmer as the temperature around them rose with the billowing steam, flowed down his body.

She looked at him wickedly. "I could get very drunk doing this." She kissed away the clear red streaks on his shoulders.

"Then I might have to take advantage of you," he answered, his voice as thick and rich as the wine.

She licked the drops clinging to his nipples. "Wasn't that the plan from the start?"

His reply was a groan as she drank the wine trailing down his abdomen. A few errant drops on his hips made her stray, but then she resumed moving downward until she found the last of the wine clinging to his erection.

"Yes, yes," he groaned.

Knowing this pleased him urged her on. He'd brought her to the brink of delight and beyond. He'd forced her to acknowledge the power and ecstasy of surrender. Now she could do the same for him. She cupped and caressed him, loved and adored him with her hands, her fingers, her mouth, her tongue.

"Enough." His words entreated and promised. "For now."

Green irises, darkly intense, held her still when he dipped his head and took her lips with his. More potent than the wine around them, his kiss drugged her. She couldn't move away, protest or even breathe. She took her sustenance from him, deeply and with all her might.

He knelt with her. The water, still steaming hot and tinted red and amber with wine and candlelight, swirled around their thighs. When he moved, little waves lapped at her like his tongue had, and the sensation made her weak.

"Jack." She snaked her hands over him, kneading her fingers into the blondish-brown hair on his chest.

He took a soft cloth from the corner of the tub, immersed it in the water and then bathed her in the wet warmth.

"It won't be long now, angel." He cupped her breasts with the cloth, then swirled the moisture around them with a loving appreciation she could see in his eyes and feel in his touch. He hadn't said the words, but then, neither had she. There'd be time enough for words. In the morning. During the next week. For the rest of their lives.

She lifted her arms for him, turning and moving so he could cleanse her. The soft roughness of the terry cloth smoothed by his attentive hands kept her skin alive, her desire primed.

After he had washed the remnants of the wine away, she took the cloth and returned the favor, kissing and touching softly and passionately until he lifted her in his arms and carried her out of the tub.

He toweled her dry and wrapped the large bath sheet around her, hooking it between her breasts and kissing the skin there to seal the lock. Taking her hand, he led her from the bathroom's steamy atmosphere to the crisp coolness of the bedroom suite.

"It seems like years since I've made love to you." He reclined on the bed, taking her with him.

She lay atop him and could feel the hardness of his desire against her belly. "Then let's not wait a minute more."

He tore the towel away and rolled her over, covering her mouth with his. His wine-sweetened tongue thrust into her mouth boldly, nearly stealing her breath with his need.

His rhythm in the tub had been slow, luxurious, savoring. Angela gasped at the sudden frantic change but matched him touch for touch and kiss for kiss. She lost herself in a multicolored delirium as he suckled her neck, laved her breasts and eased her legs apart with his knees to dip his fingers inside her until she pooled slick and ready.

"No more, Jack. I want you inside me. Now."

He responded quickly, stopping only to slip on a condom before he plunged inside. She lifted her hips, accepting the full length of him, encouraging him to love her to the core. She needed no more teasing. She needed only him.

His strokes were rhythmic, deep and long. She met each thrust, giving a little of herself and gaining a part of him. His pace increased. The sensations came in rapid succession. She didn't know where one started and the other ended.

But she didn't care. His loving was like a safety net, ready to catch her and giving her confidence to jump again and again. They clutched each other and kissed each other until the air exploded around them. When the eruptions subsided, they touched and soothed and kissed until they fell, weak and sated, into a deep sleep.

BEFORE THE SUN ROSE over the eastern horizon, Angela awoke and checked the clock. Her body, slowed by a delicious ache, barely cooperated as she grabbed her sandals by the straps, draped her dress and underthings over her arm, kissed Jack on the cheek as he slept and returned to her room.

She'd been in her bed for less than an hour when the

sun came up. Sleep came in uneven snatches, mixed with the luscious memories of their lovemaking. They'd come together more times than she'd thought possible, each time fulfilling another fantasy and reaching a higher plateau. By the time they'd finally fallen asleep, each knew every inch of the other's body.

And possibly every measure of the other's soul.

When Dani knocked on her door at seven-thirty, wide-awake and ready to attack the day with a nine-year-old's enthusiasm, Angela couldn't help falling into a vibrant mood.

And why not? Today, she'd tell Jack the truth.

She showered and dressed, amazed she hadn't considered this particular scenario before. She'd been so tied up in the past, she'd failed to see the possibilities for the future. If Jack loved her as she suspected, she and Dani could look forward to a lifetime of commitment and caring.

Jack went to the main house and had a picnic breakfast packed by the time she had Dani dressed. Dani insisted they eat in transit, and Jack cheerfully concurred. Though Angela felt no need to argue, she wondered how many times she'd succumb to this invincible tag team. She loved them both so much. For once, she looked forward to losing.

The cemetery, located a mile outside Castiloga, burgeoned with draping trees and stone paths. Though not large, the memorial garden housed over a hundred of the local deceased, with some tombstones dating back to the early eighteen hundreds. A local winemaker who knew Chryssie had offered a space in his family plot. At the time, Angela had reservations about accepting. Yet every time she passed through the tall wrought-iron gates, she remembered why she'd said yes. Serenity,

history and beauty mingled here like seashells and sea-
weed on a white-sanded shore.

Angela leaned toward the front seat, pointing out
where to park. As he eased the convertible into the
space, Dani gasped.

"The flowers! We forgot to pick flowers!"

Angela touched her daughter on the shoulder. "We'll
come back again before we leave, sweetie. We'll bring
flowers then."

Dani's frown deepened. "It's still early. Let's go
back."

"Hey," Jack interrupted, his voice calm and hushed.
"I saw a roadside stand on our way here. Why don't
you go on ahead and I'll go buy some."

"Would you?" Dani's smile rivaled the morning sun.
"Pick pretty ones. Mama liked red, okay?"

She threw open the car door and skipped up the path,
not looking to see if Angela followed.

Laying her hand on Jack's shoulder as thanks, Angela
got out of the car. She walked slowly, prepared to allow
Dani ample time alone at her mother's grave. She usually didn't intrude until shortly before they left.

Angela scanned the landscape for Mr. Davis, the
cemetery's caretaker. She found him about fifty yards
away, armed with his rake, tending the graves nestled
under a sprawling willow. He shielded his eyes with
his hand, then smiled in recognition. Angela waved, sat
down and pulled a book of poetry Chryssie had left her
from her purse. After spotting Dani yanking a weed
from beside Chryssie's memorial and chattering with
her usual animated excitement, she let contentment
ease over her. She opened the book and began to read.

JACK BOUGHT two dozen roses at the roadside stand
then hurried to the car. He smiled and laid the flowers

carefully on the seat, replaying the look on Dani's face when he'd offered to get them. The delight in her sea-green eyes warmed him to the marrow. When was the last time he'd felt such gratification from a smile?

Last night. With Angela.

Of course, he reasoned as he retraced the road to the cemetery, the reactions differed greatly. He'd been miffed about Angela's keeping Dani a secret, but now he knew her reasons. The child inspired similar protec-tiveness in him. Without a doubt, he'd do anything to make the munchkin happy.

He parked in the same spot as before, debated, then decided to leave the top down on such a clear morning. He stepped out of the car and scanned the cemetery for signs of Angela and Dani.

"They're down over that hill a bit," a voice volun-teered.

Turning, he found himself greeted warmly by a wiz-ened old man with a rake.

"Thanks."

"I'm Sam Davis. I take care of this place."

After the man extracted his hand from a thick gar-dening glove, Jack shook it.

"Jack Sullivan."

The man's liquid gray eyes narrowed, then bright-ened as if he recognized Jack from somewhere.

"Well, I'll be. I wondered when the father would get himself up here."

"The father?" Jack pulled his hand away, unsure if the shaking he felt came from him or Mr. Davis.

"I was here when they laid Miss Chryssie down." He balanced his rake against his thigh and shoved his gloves into the pocket of his grass-stained coat. "That little angel of hers near about broke my heart, being so strong and brave. I look forward to her visit every year. Miss Angela pays me extra to make sure the grave is nicely tended all year round."

"The father?" Jack repeated.

Davis eyed him warily. "Don't tell me I'm mistaken. I've seen hundreds of relations tracking up and down these hills. Miss Chryssie's picture is on her headstone. I see both of you in that little girl as plain as I see the sun in the sky."

Jack's chest tightened. Bile rose in his throat. He jerked around, searching for Dani, needing to look at her one more time and then knowing he really didn't have to.

12

"WHEN WERE YOU going to tell me?"

Angela dropped her book, startled by the knife-edge tone of Jack's voice. He'd approached with the stealth of a starved tiger. The ferocity in his eyes heightened the comparison.

He knew.

Just in case, she feigned confusion. "What are you talking about, Jack?"

He snatched her arm above the elbow and yanked her until they were nearly eye-to-eye. Angela tossed a cautious glance over her shoulder, hoping Dani hadn't seen. When he caught her movement, he loosened his grip. But not by much.

"You heard me, Angela. When were you going to tell me that Dani is my daughter?"

Through tight teeth, the question seethed with anger. His grip, slowly increasing in pressure from clamp to vise, cut off her circulation. She struggled against the pain.

"Last night. This morning. When I knew you wouldn't take her. When I thought you'd stay."

He released her quickly and took two steps back, breathing raggedly, staring into the distance where Dani knelt beside Chryssie's grave talking nonstop and giggling at a scampering squirrel. His eyes became liquid and his clenched jaw quivered. His hands were fists at his side.

Angela snatched off her sunglasses and waited, swallowing to dispel the lump in her throat, willing her bottom lip to stop shaking. How could she have done this to him? In all the years she'd known him, she never remembered seeing such fury. Such agony. She folded the sunglasses and clutched them in her hand. She heard the plastic frames crack. Slowly, she lowered herself to the bench, waiting for him to speak.

In the span of his silent rage, Dani caught sight of him, waved, then scurried across the lawn, thwarting their discussion.

"Did you bring the flowers?" She climbed into Angela's lap as if she was still a toddler.

"Two dozen." When he spoke to her, his voice softened. His hands relaxed. His smile came involuntarily. He couldn't help staring at her, scrutinizing her features, comparing them to his. "Mr. Davis offered to get water for the vase."

She'd hooked her hands around Angela's neck and looked at him beneath caramel-colored lashes. Her round green eyes, shaped like his, tugged at him with a force he'd never known before.

He had a child. The realization would have taken his breath away right there had he not known to hide this from Dani until he was sure.

God, how he envied Angela, holding Dani so lovingly.

And how he resented her for keeping this secret.

"I'll go get them," Angela volunteered.

"No, let me. I want to show Mr. Davis the statue I made at camp for Mom." Angela released her with a kiss on the cheek.

Once Dani had crossed to the other side of the walkway, Jack attempted to hang on to the comfort and contentment Dani inspired. It wasn't easy. She was his, wasn't she?

"How recently did you know?" He started the conversation with no hesitation. He'd always believed Angela to be the one innately honest person he knew. He prayed she wouldn't let him down now, though he already knew she had.

"Do you mean how recently did I suspect Dani was your daughter or how recently did I suspect Chryssie lied to me about the real identity of Dani's biological father?"

He nodded, realizing the deception had to lead back to Chryssie. The night they'd been together had been a fluke—a mistake made by two hyper-hormonal teenagers who'd had too much to drink. Yet if Dani was the product of this brief liaison, he had a right to know.

"What did Chryssie tell you?"

"She didn't tell me a thing." Angela swiped away an errant lock of auburn hair. "She let me believe Richard Lassiter was the baby's father, but as far as she was concerned, the baby was hers and hers alone. She forbade me to ever mention him."

"What about the birth certificate?" He kept his voice calm, rational, hoping his heart would follow suit.

"She left the father part blank and set up a will naming me as guardian. I was in college and already working. I didn't question her. She seemed to be doing all the right things."

He shoved his hands into his pockets and clutched the material inside. "Keeping a baby's existence from its father was the right thing?"

She bit her bottom lip and turned away.

The question had come out with more anger than he'd intended. He hadn't been there. He had no right to judge. He calmed himself with a deep breath. "When did you realize Richard wasn't the father?"

"About two years ago, Dani became very ill." She drew her leg underneath her and shifted uncomfortably. "She had a mild case of hepatitis, but for a while, I worried she suffered from something genetic, something she might need a donor for, or medical information from a blood relative. I decided to search for Richard then, against Chryssie's wishes."

"She was gone by then."

"Chryssie is never gone from our lives, Jack." Her tone resonated with frustration and sadness. "She's Dani's mother. I had to try to respect her wishes. She left me a letter asking me not to look for Dani's father until Dani was eighteen, and then only if Dani wanted to know more about him."

Jack heard the anguish and regret in Angela's voice. This wasn't any easier for her than for him. Only hours before, they'd touched each other with the abandon of soul mates, pleased each other like lovers possessed. He'd come so close to admitting how much he loved her, to asking her to refuse Davenport's offer for no other reason than to become his wife. How could so much change in so little time?

"But you changed your mind."

"Dani's health had to come first. As soon as she recovered, I found Richard."

Jack nodded, unable to say anything. The tale was complex. More than just lies or truths. Still, his blood simmered. Angela had withheld this from him willfully.

He should have been angry enough to murder her.

Instead, he fought the impulse to kiss her until the torment vanished from her eyes.

"I met with Richard and his wife to gauge their interest in children before I spilled the beans. But his wife beat me to it. Seems they'd been trying to adopt a baby since they'd been married. Richard was sterile. He always had been."

"That's when you suspected me?"

Angela stared at him with disbelief. "Why would I do that, Jack? You were *my* boyfriend, remember? As far as I knew, you and Chryssie didn't even get along."

He held up his hand in brief surrender. "I'm sorry."

She sat up straight and avoided the subject of her personal pain. "I suspected you only after I'd exhausted every possibility. I reread Chryssie's diary and the old notes we used to pass during chemistry. I tracked down a friend of hers who lived down the street. No one knew of anyone but Richard. Chryssie talked a good game, but she didn't sleep around like people thought.

"Then I found *my* old diary. Around prom time, I'd made a lot of entries about how I felt when you left me at the dance, how Richard had driven me home."

Jack sat back and crossed his arms over his chest. He didn't like hearing her version of one of the worst nights of his life. Especially not when he'd come so far in making up for his mistake.

"Chryssie never told you what happened?" he asked, wanting to get through the story with maximum speed.

"Chryssie was my friend. She wouldn't deliberately hurt me, and if she did, she'd do her damnedest to cover it up. She told me you'd given her a ride home and that she'd bitched at you for dumping me. Now I know that isn't exactly how the conversation must have gone."

He watched as Angela chewed her bottom lip and rubbed her palms together. He'd dredged up myriad bad memories, for her and for him. He wanted to take her hands in his and calm them with a gentle squeeze. But he wasn't sure he could be gentle.

Instead, he stepped closer. "So if you never knew from Chryssie, why'd you suspect me?"

She scooted on the bench, increasing the distance between them. "About six months ago, after I put two and two together, I counted back nine months from Dani's birthday to prom night. Then, for the first time, I looked at Dani's eyes, at the texture of her hair, the shape of her jawline. I mean *really* looked. The resemblance is undeniable."

"Is that why you came to the reunion? To find her father?"

She clipped her sunglasses onto the neckline of her blouse and shook her head. "Dani didn't have anything to do with my wanting to be with you. She was the reason I wanted to *not* be with you—the reason I wanted to get you out of my system once and for all." She looked into her lap, then around her, as if searching for some elusive guidance. "After ten years, I couldn't get you out of my heart. And I needed to so badly."

Her straightforwardness disarmed him. He sat beside her, not too close, leaned forward on his elbows and laid his head in his hands. He had a daughter. A lovely one. A bright ray of sunshine with a love for sports and an appreciation for beauty.

And she had a mother who didn't want to love him.

He looked up, knowing his eyes betrayed his hurt. "So you decided to lie, thinking a brief, meaningless affair would justify keeping me in the dark? She's my daughter, dammit."

"I didn't think you'd want her to be. I love her. I'd protect her with my life. I couldn't let you know her if I thought you'd abandon her like your father abandoned you. Or if I thought your visits would take place in the company of skinny, vapid fashion-model wannabes and their sleazoid agents."

"So you did read the rags," Jack spat.

"Behind every rumor is an inkling of truth. You can't deny that."

He shook his head. "No, but you wouldn't believe which parts were true and which were false."

He moved on the bench, closing in on her, needing her nearness. His ire cooled when the hem of her skirt brushed against his hand. Her reasons, no matter how distressing to him, were grounded in a stalwart obligation to protect her child—possibly his child.

But her doubts still stabbed him like a stake through his heart.

"I'd believe anything you told me. I'd believe now," she whispered. Her glossy gaze captured him, shackling his heart like iron. When she touched his hand, his mind shot to the night before—to the intimacy they'd shared. He'd spent the entire week teaching her to trust him. Had he failed entirely?

Maybe today was his turn to trust.

"You weren't the only one with regrets about our past." Jack closed his hand over hers lightly, afraid she'd pull away if he held on too tight. "I've wondered what if quite a few times myself. And I had more what ifs to answer. Chryssie and I were drunk. I was never even sure how far we went that night, but I knew we'd betrayed you and that I could never try to get you back. If you had found out—"

Her fingers tensed. "You two must have sworn a pact."

"We never said a word to each other. After I took her home, I don't think we spoke again. Ever."

Angela nodded. She knew the truth without doubt, and still the pain was dulled. Knowing that Dani resulted from their tryst eased the betrayal.

"I guess hate and love walk a fine parallel line."

"Hate and *lust*," he clarified. "Besides, I never hated Chryssie. She just got on my nerves because she was so close to you. I didn't need her bad-mouthing me at every opportunity."

Angela chuckled quietly. "That she did. She insisted I couldn't handle a cad like you."

"A *cad?* Interesting word. I think the tabloid press used it when they reported I'd dumped Lily Dee."

"Why did you dump her?"

"I didn't. That's just what her publicist told the press. Lily left me shortly after she discovered she was pregnant."

The chill snaking up Angela's spine had nothing to do with the cold air, already dispelling under the morning sun. Did Dani have a little half brother or half sister somewhere in the world? She'd never considered, never asked.

"Don't worry, angel," he said, spying her wide-eyed stare, "I haven't turned into my father yet. I'm not indiscriminately spreading my seed all over the Western Hemisphere."

She swallowed before she spoke. A protective numbness settled over her. "Then she wasn't really pregnant?"

He looked away, staring at the distant gravestones blankly. His Adam's apple bobbed as he choked back a strong wave of emotion. His eyes flashed with renewed rage and well-rooted regret.

"After she left, she wasn't."

His gaze met hers straight on, and his implication was clear. Then the sadness she'd glimpsed slipped under the surface of his stoic expression.

"Lily denied everything, so I'll never know for sure. But suspecting was enough to convince me my life didn't mean much. I loved my work, but not my life. I didn't know what to do. Until I received an invitation to the reunion."

And he'd come home to an even bigger lie than the one he'd left.

"I wanted to start over, find the kind of life I'd never had with my parents. A life based on loyalty, honesty and children." He leaned back on the bench and raked his hands through his hair. "And all you wanted was to get me out of your system."

Frustration propelled her to stand. "I had to erase you from my dreams. You'd slept with my best friend." Her words choked her. "I kept telling myself I was being ridiculous, holding on to puppy love."

"You don't listen to yourself very well."

"No, I don't." She stopped before the anger churning in her stomach bubbled to the surface. Rationalizing didn't help. Reminding herself that she loved him didn't, either. That made it worse. He made her so damn mad.

"You want to know why I pursued you even when I realized you might be Dani's father? I weighed one problem against the other. If you were her father, I was going to have to make serious decisions about her future. I couldn't be wrong. I told myself I wouldn't be able to be objective about Dani if I still..."

His expression hardened, along with the tone of his voice. "If you still what?"

She hunted for a phrase, a powerful one, a grouping of words she simply couldn't speak aloud. She loved him. Perhaps she always had. Yet for Dani's sake, she couldn't say it. The force of the admission could jeopardize her control over Dani's future—something she was not yet willing to relinquish.

"If I still desired you to the point of distraction." She recognized his disappointment. Shifting uncomfortably, she sat and laid her hand beside his in an imperfect gesture of apology. "When the reunion came up, I devised my asinine plan. The minute I laid eyes on you, I knew I was in trouble. You never make anything easy."

"Nope," he verified, twining her fingers with his. A pensive smile tilted the corners of his mouth, then disappeared. "I told you I wanted to see if we could cross the lines of passion together. What I didn't tell you is that I knew from the start we would. That wasn't why I made the challenge."

"Then why did you?"

He released her hand with a reluctance that tugged at her heart. She moved forward on the bench, wanting to touch him, to ease away the deep lines creasing his face.

"You didn't trust me. You can't love someone you don't trust. I've learned that the hard way. Haven't you?"

ANGELA FLIPPED through the channels, barely registering the cacophony coming from the television. Her gaze never wandered from the portable phone on the table. Jack's lawyer had called the day before, informing her the test results would be in this afternoon. They'd call

Jack first, of course, but then he'd channel the information to her through the attorney. Only when she gave the go-ahead would Jack contact her.

Communication between them had been sparse since they'd returned from California. After their discussion at the graveyard, Jack decided to head to Monterey to visit his father, though Angela suspected he simply wanted to escape. She returned the favor by absenting herself from the photo shoots for Whispering Palms. He needed time and space to think. She didn't blame him.

But she missed him.

Angela tried to throw herself into her work, but found no pleasure in it, even after David Styler came crawling back. He'd heard she might be able to convince Jack Sullivan to photograph his next collection, which remarkably had a nature theme. She made no promises but took Styler's account to motivate her staff, who'd been disappointed when she declined Davenport's offer. She couldn't help thinking how Jack would have been pleased—*would* being the key word.

Turning off the television and tossing the remote control on the nearest pillow, she untucked her legs from beneath her and stretched. The hall clock tolled twice. She cradled her head in her hands. How much longer could she possibly wait?

She hoped the news confirmed her suspicions about Jack. Not just because he'd be a good father but because she wanted him in her life. She almost didn't care if he hated her so long as he felt something. She'd have to work from there.

Whether or not they could salvage their relationship remained to be seen. She'd acted as any fiercely independent single mother would, with Dani's best interests at the forefront. But her actions hurt Jack, and he was one to hold onto his wounds. He dealt with them well, but he never forgot them.

The sliding glass door to the backyard slid open, and Dani slipped in, jumping when she spotted Angela on the couch.

"Dani? Where've you been? I thought you were in your room playing your new video game."

Dani turned her oversize baseball cap backward and shoved her hands into the pockets of her shorts.

"I was. I mean, I went to show Christopher and Vincent. I learned how to get to a new level."

Angela nodded and sat against the cushions, wishing they would provide some comfort for her aching back. She considered taking a swim to relieve her knotted muscles, but she didn't want to be in the pool when the call came.

Dani took Angela's silence as a dismissal, but she only walked to the threshold before turning back.

"Mom?"

The worried look on the child's face evoked an increase in Angela's already rapidly beating heart. "What is it, hon?"

Dani took her cap off and laid it on the nearest chair, then climbed onto the couch beside Angela. Instinctively, Angela opened her arms and Dani curled into her embrace. She stroked the child's blond hair, enjoying the feel of her in her arms. As Dani grew, these moments became rarer, though not as much as she imagined they would once puberty hit.

"Do you love Jack?"

Angela stopped her petting. "What makes you ask?"

Dani shrugged. "I dunno. You haven't been very happy since he left. I figured you missed him."

Tightening her hold, Angela tilted her head against

Dani's, breathing in the apple scent of her recently washed hair.

"Yeah, I guess I do. Miss him, I mean."

"But you don't love him?"

She cleared her throat. She'd never lied to Dani before, and the question seemed too direct to ignore.

"Well, honey, with adults, things aren't always as simple as one person being in love with another person."

"I think he loves you back," Dani assured her.

"Oh, do you? And how do you know so much about love, huh?" She held Dani at arm's length. "You better slow down, young lady. I'm not ready to see you off on your first date just yet."

"Gross." Dani crinkled her nose like a coquettish kitten. "I'm not gonna have a date! But I think you could use some."

"Danae Hart Harris, have you been talking to Aunt Kelly?"

"Not about dates."

"Then what made you think about this nonsense? You don't have to worry about me or my love life. And neither do I." She enclosed Dani in her arms again. "I have more important things to worry about right now."

"Like if Jack is my real dad?"

The question stopped her cold. Dani broke their hug.

"Who told you that?" Angela asked, her voice barely audible.

"Nobody. I figured it out."

"I didn't know you even wondered about your father."

Dani pushed her hair out of her face and dangled her legs over the edge of the couch. "I always wonder about him."

"Always?" Why hadn't she realized?

"I kept thinking he'd find me one day. And, well, I sort of look like Jack. I mean—" she dug into her pocket for a wallet-size photo taken at one of the novelty booths at Pizza Palace "—we look alike, don't we?"

Angela took the picture lovingly, cupping it in the palm of her hand and switching on the table lamp. Two pairs of eyes, perfectly oval and glittering green, stared at her. Though Dani did favor Chryssie's coloring, she had Jack's cheekbones and chin. Even the contours of their foreheads were similar. She tried not to compare the smiles, both equally broad and touching every inch of their faces. They'd only known each other for a couple of hours when the picture was taken, and still the bond between parent and child had begun to form. Angela knew the feeling. She'd experienced a similar one shortly after she'd first held Dani in her arms.

"Yeah, honey, I guess you do."

"Then he is my dad?" The question was uncertain, unsure, as if she feared a negative answer.

"The truth is, I don't know. I'm waiting by the phone to find out. Jack took some tests. The doctors are comparing his DNA to yours, and that'll tell us if he's your father. They'll call us when they know."

Dani eyed the phone and then nodded.

"Mom?"

"Yes, sweetie?"

"It doesn't matter."

"What doesn't?"

"If he's my dad. I mean, if he's *really* my dad."

"Unfortunately, it does matter." She handed the photo to Dani, who put it in her pocket.

"To who? Not to Jack."

"And how do you know that?" Dani's blush pointed

Angela toward the truth. "Have you talked to Jack about this?"

"Not about him being my dad, or not being. We just talked about you. I got tired of you looking so sad."

"I don't look sad."

Dani rolled her eyes and smirked. "Hello? Yes, Mom, you do. And when I told Aunt Kelly yesterday, she said I oughta do something to cheer you up."

"So you called Jack." She wasn't surprised Kelly had a hand in this. Despite her reservations about Angela's association with Jack, her sister was a born romantic. "How did you find his number?"

Dani's grin denoted guilt, but the twinkle in her eyes showed pride in her resourcefulness. "Well, you had his business card in your planner."

Grabbing her purse, Angela found her wallet. Before she could open the section where she kept her business cards, Dani removed the crinkled card from her pocket.

"Danae, this is serious. You're not supposed to sneak into my things."

"I know, but this was important. You love him, Mom. Even if he isn't my dad, you love him. I can tell."

"So you snuck over to Aunt Kelly's and called to tell him?"

"Sort of, and to ask him to come over so he could fix whatever made you have a fight."

"Oh, Dani." Angela pressed her hands against her forehead. "There's so much you don't understand, that you can't understand."

"And why can't she?" Jack asked, entering stealthily from the front hall. "She seems like a brilliant young lady to me."

Dani blushed again, and Angela's heart slammed against her chest. She hadn't seen him in nearly two weeks, and the minute she set eyes on him, she realized how she'd missed the sound of his voice, the compassion in his gaze, and the little half smile tilting the corner of his mouth.

"Jack, I—" She stuttered and stopped, knowing the words couldn't come.

Dani slid off the couch and went to stand at Jack's side. He ran his hand lovingly over the top of her blond head, and she smiled at him with a beam Angela had never seen before.

Turning to her mother, Dani waited. At first, her smile lasted. But soon her look showed exasperation.

"Mo-ther?"

Dani shuffled over and grabbed Angela's hand, pulling her from the couch. Only when she'd positioned her mother a few inches away from Jack did she back up to watch from the doorway.

"Jack, I'm sorry about what I did," Angela confessed, feeling an enormous weight lift from her heart. She glanced at Dani, and urged by her daughter's brilliantly lit face, took Jack's hand in hers. "I do trust you. I guess I was just afraid to trust myself."

Jack ran his palm along her cheek, then crooked his finger beneath her chin and tilted her face so he could gaze fully into her eyes.

"We're both afraid. But fear loves company, especially the company of the people you love."

"I do love you, Jack. I always have. That's why I couldn't get you out of my mind. I don't think my finding you at the reunion had to do with any other reason."

He kissed her, unmindful of Dani's girlish giggle or the beating of his heart or the chirping sound echoing in his brain. He knew nothing else but the sweet, soft feel of her lips pressed to his, needing and wanting him with no reservation.

Only when Dani said hello into the phone did they both pull away.

"Just a moment, please." She turned and handed the cordless phone to Jack.

He stood silent, then clamped his hand over the mouthpiece.

"Marry me."

Her breath caught in her throat. She and Dani both said, "What?" at the same time.

Jack's grin spread across his whole face. He got down on one knee, balanced the phone over his thigh and took Angela's fingers in one hand, Dani's in the other.

"The results of this test aren't important. I want you to marry me. Please."

Angela looked into her daughter's eyes, unable to speak as she caught Dani's love for Jack mirrored there.

She managed a nod.

He kissed her hand, then Dani's, and took the call.

Angela took Dani by the shoulders, bracing herself and the child for the information to come. Then she relaxed and smiled, remembering the gentle sensation of his lips crushed against hers. He wanted her. Not just for one night or one weekend, but a lifetime. And even better, she wanted him, too.

Jack pushed the button that disconnected the call and tossed the phone onto the couch with a whoop.

"Looks like we have a match!" He slapped his hands together and opened his arms to Dani.

Dani yahooed and leaped into Jack's embrace. "Looks like I've got a dad!"

He twirled Dani twice, and Angela could only step back and surrender to the tears spilling from her eyes.

When they stopped spinning, Jack and Dani shanghaied Angela into their hug.

Angela reveled in the giddiness of Dani's laugh and the warm protectiveness of Jack's arms locked around them both. They loved each other. He loved Dani. Dani loved him. In her deepest dreams, she couldn't have hoped for more.

She stepped back, though not out of the circle of their arms, and assessed them as a fat tear splashed down her face.

"Looks like we have a family."

Angela pressed her face against Jack's denim shirt, inhaling his woodsy scent and loving how her tears melded into his skin. When Dani squirmed from between them, Jack pulled Angela closer, sealing the gesture with a crowning kiss.

"Aunt Kelly's gonna love this!" Dani threw open the sliding glass door and raced across the yard without a backward glance.

"You do realize she's gonna be a handful," Angela warned, snuggling her face so tightly to his chest, she felt the imprint of his buttons on her cheek.

Jack lowered his hands from her shoulders to her hips, loosening his bear hug just enough to gaze at her with his devastating emerald eyes. The longing she'd come to anticipate, the need she'd come to crave, stared at her with unchained clarity. His eyes radiated love and passion—all-encompassing and all for her.

Jack grinned. "I should be surprised? Her mother's been a handful for as long as I've known her."

"You ain't seen nothing yet, Sullivan." Rising on her tiptoes, she kissed his jawline, flicking her smooth tongue over his rough stubble, blowing a cool breath against the lingering moisture.

His chuckle rumbled like distant thunder. "Aren't you done seducing me yet, angel?"

She slipped her hands into the back pockets of his jeans.

"I'll never be done seducing you, Sullivan. Not in this lifetime."

He cupped her bottom and pressed her forward, crushing her hips to his. He was hard against her belly. His eyes darkened. Her breath caught.

"I'm going to hold you to your promise, angel." He dipped his head and nibbled the base of her neck. "Forever."

'HAVE I DONE something wrong?' Angie persisted, wishing Taylor would emit a sense of camaraderie instead of holding an impenetrable reserve.

'Not at all,' he assured her. 'I would say a lot of things right. You seem to be fitting into our little Outback community very well. I've heard only good things about you.'

'They're nice people,' she said sincerely. Only the Maguire family kept her shut out of their hearts.

'Yes,' he agreed. 'Though I appreciate it's taken considerable effort from you. It is a world away from what you're used to.'

The control Angie had been exerting over her feelings snapped. He wasn't as blatant as his aunt in his prejudice against her but she'd felt it coming through every word he'd spoken and she didn't deserve any of it.

'Don't judge me by your wife!'

His jaw jerked. A flicker of some dark emotion destroyed the steady power of his probing gaze.

'No two people are the same. If you don't know that, you're a man of very limited vision. So I come from the city as your wife did! That doesn't stop me from being an individual in my own right.'

She straightened up, proudly defiant, furiously angry with the situation. 'I'm *me*. Angie Cordell. And it's time you took the blinkers off your eyes, Taylor Maguire.'

Then she whirled away from him, too agitated by the explosive expulsion of her emotion to keep facing him.

The storm outside hadn't yet eased. There was nowhere to go. She stopped at the window, staring blindly at the torrential rain. The thundering on the roof was almost deafening but it wasn't as loud as the silence behind her.

'You want me to go, don't you? You've given me a month's respite and now you want me to leave and channel my energies somewhere else.'

'I didn't say that, Angie.'

'You were working your way around it.' Bitterness at his tactics spewed the suspicion. 'Do you have your first choice of governess waiting in the wings?'

'No. I said I'd give you a chance.'

'Have you?' She swung around to face him. 'Have you really, Taylor?'

He hadn't moved. He didn't move now except to make a gesture of appeasement. 'Angie, I was merely trying to ascertain how you felt.'

'Then let me tell you your cynicism was shining through every word.'

He frowned, shook his head. 'I didn't mean to hurt you.' The blue eyes fastened on hers with devastating sincerity. 'I truly did not come in here to take you down or suggest you leave.'

Her heart jiggled painfully. He might be speaking the truth but the judgements were still there, the judgements that ruled his attitude towards her, that kept her shut out of his life, denied any real sharing with him, denied his confidence and trust. She didn't know why it meant so much to her but it did. It did. And the need to fight for justice from him was as much a raging torrent inside her as the rain outside.

It's hot...
and it's out of control!

This summer, Temptation turns up the heat.
Look for these bold, provocative,
ultra-sexy books!

#686 SEDUCING SULLIVAN
Julie Elizabeth Leto
June 1998

Angela Harris had only one obsession—Jack Sullivan.
Ever since high school, he'd been on her mind...and
in her fantasies. But no more. At her ten-year
reunion, she was going to get him out of her system
for good. All she needed was one sizzling night with
Jack—and then she could get on with her life.
Unfortunately she hadn't counted on Jack having a
few obsessions of his own....

BLAZE! Red-hot reads from

MEN *at* WORK

All work and no play? Not these men!

April 1998

KNIGHT SPARKS by Mary Lynn Baxter

Sexy lawman Rance Knight made a career of arresting the bad guys. Somehow, though, he thought policewoman Carly Mitchum was framed. Once they'd uncovered the truth, could Rance let Carly go...or would he make a citizen's arrest?

May 1998

HOODWINKED by Diana Palmer

CEO Jake Edwards donned coveralls and went undercover as a mechanic to find the saboteur in his company. Nothing—or no one—would distract him, not even beautiful secretary Maureen Harris. Jake had to catch the thief—*and* the woman who'd stolen his heart!

June 1998

DEFYING GRAVITY by Rachel Lee

Tim O'Shaughnessy and his business partner, Liz Pennington, had always been close—but never *this* close. As the danger of their assignment escalated, so did their passion. When the job was over, could they ever go back to business as usual?

MEN AT WORK™

Available at your favorite retail outlet!

 HARLEQUIN®   Silhouette®

Not The Same Old Story!

 Exciting, glamorous
romance stories that take
readers around the world.

 Sparkling, fresh and ten-
der love stories that
bring you pure romance.

Bold and adventurous—
Temptation is strong women,
bad boys, great sex!

HARLEQUIN SUPERROMANCE® Provocative and realistic
stories that celebrate life
and love.

 Contemporary
fairy tales—where
anything is possible
and where dreams
come true.

HARLEQUIN®
INTRIGUE® Heart-stopping, suspenseful
adventures that combine the
best of romance and mystery.

 Humorous and romantic stories
that capture the lighter side of
love.

Heat up your summer this July with

Summer Lovers

This July, bestselling authors Barbara Delinsky,
Elizabeth Lowell and Anne Stuart present three
couples with pasts that threaten their future happiness.
Can they play with fire without being burned?

FIRST, BEST AND ONLY
by Barbara Delinsky

GRANITE MAN
by Elizabeth Lowell

CHAIN OF LOVE
by Anne Stuart

Available wherever Harlequin and Silhouette books
are sold.

HARLEQUIN®

Silhouette®

HARLEQUIN®

Temptation®

COMING NEXT MONTH

#689 BLACK VELVET Carrie Alexander
Blaze

Journalist Thomas Jericho was determined to discover the true identity of Madame X, author of the wildly successful and erotic Black Velvet books. Shy librarian Amalie Dove was equally determined to keep her wild side a secret, but Jericho was relentless…and Amalie was in love….

#690 THE NAKED TRUTH Dani Sinclair

Brenna Wolford liked adventure—but even *she* had to admit that breaking and entering was a little extreme. Unfortunately, her grandfather's life depended on her finding a forged painting before the authorities did. But the last thing she expected to encounter was another thief! Especially a sexy rogue intent on stealing both the art…and her heart!

#691 THE LONE WOLF Sandy Steen
Mail Order Men

Torn between two lovers? Cowboy Reese Barrett put his ad in *Texas Men* magazine, never dreaming he'd find a woman like Natalie. But just when he was ready to meet her, gorgeous Shea Alexander arrived at the ranch and sent Reese's libido working overtime. How could he choose between them?

#692 THE WRONG MAN IN WYOMING Kristine Rolofson
Boots & Booties

The last thing Jed Monroe wanted on his ranch was a beautiful woman and her children, but before he knew it he'd hired Abby Andrews as his cook and was getting up at night to soothe her baby's cries. And that's not all he wanted to do late at night…. Not when he looked into Abby's eyes, pulled her close and thought about *never* letting her go….

AVAILABLE NOW: